Chapter 1

On a cool Alabama morning in 1978, two days before Christmas, Jake Keller sits at the breakfast table.

"Daddy, Daddy," his daughter Megan yells with excitement. "Can I pull the next paper ring? There's only two more days till Santa comes."

"Of course, you can, sweetie," Jake replies as he smiles at his wife, Christine.

Christine and Jake have been married for three years but had dated for what they say was most of their lives. Megan is almost four years old and has the spirit of the wind. Although some disapproved, Jake and Christine knew they would love each other forever and just figured they'd get married when the time was right.

As breakfast wraps up, Jake grabs his coat. "Well, I better be off. Don't wanna get fired already." It was his first month on the job as a police officer.

Christine laughed. "Okay, well, you better make sure Santa doesn't have any problems out there. Wouldn't want him getting in trouble for going down those chimneys."

D1528534

"Mom," Megan replied, with a sassy look.

"Okay, okay. Go on, sweetie. Get ready for the day."

Megan ran to Jake, gave him a big hug, and turned to the stairs.

Jake and Christine said their goodbyes, and he was on his way.

*****

As he drives down Main Street, he waves to all the folks shopping and getting breakfast. He nods to Mr. Hindle at the gas station and finally pulls into his parking spot. The police station is old but clean. Most of the staff are friendly, and the noise of typing and the smell of coffee fills the air. His desk is very simple. A picture of his family sits on the left, and papers stack high on the right. He sits and sips the overly burned, lukewarm coffee.

"Hey, Rook," a shout comes from across the room. "We got the big one for ya!"

Jake looks up at Vern approaching.

Vern isn't a real nice guy, and Jake is never sure if he is serious or just playing tricks half the time. Vern has been with the force for nearly twenty years and, next to the captain, pretty much runs the place.

"Oh, yeah? What's goin' on?"

"Well, your gonna come with me and the boys. We got reports that thefts have taken place down in Elmgrove. We're gonna stake it out and see what we find."

"Ha-ha, you got me. Four officers for some shoplifter?"

"Dammit, Rook. Get your shit together and be ready by eight. We're making it a late night."

Again, Jake feels embarrassed but even more frustrated. "Eight o'clock." He shakes his head, takes another sip, and organizes the papers on his desk. "This should be a great time," he whispers to himself.

*****

Elmgrove is about twenty-five miles from town. Just what Jake wants—a long ride with Vern and the other two men. Of course, Vern is driving impossibly slow. At this speed, the four may not arrive until nine.

Sam sits shotgun—the so-called second-in-command after Vern. Sam is a weathered man, always chewing or smoking. He has little remorse for the ash that flies into Jake's face. Sam doesn't talk much; at the same time, no one ever wants him to anyway. He has a way of making people feel really awkward.

Tommy sits in the back behind Vern. He's the type to go to the bar, sneak in a fifth, drink the whole damn bottle, and break shit. He has no problem flashing that badge. The captain would have thrown him out a long time ago if it wasn't for Vern. For some reason, the two are close, and Vern covers for him all the time.

They approach the town and settle in, dressed in plain clothes to fit in.

"Alright. Me and Tommy will head north. Sam, take the southeast corner. Rook, you stay here. We'll call if we need you."

Although Jake doesn't want to sit there, he is pretty happy to stay as far from them as possible. The three take off, and Jake remains in the car, laying his head on the headrest to try to steal a wink.

*****

On the other side of town, an exhausted delivery man drops off his last packages. It's always the biggest mail day of the year, and mail services need to deliver all packages before Christmas. He only has a few left and enjoys the holiday night.

*****

Meanwhile, Vern comes over the radio, "Rook, get your ass down to 217 West Breach. There's an emergency entrance in back. We got it propped open for you. Come in quiet. Be alert for anything. We got the big one."

Jake took a big deep breath and headed down the street.

*****

The delivery man has only one package left. He had to place the last few on the porches of the receiving establishments; just about everything is closed now. A few Open signs glow down the dark streets, but for every illuminated sign, five other buildings are empty, with their workers home, sharing the night with their families.

To his luck, the last stop is just ahead—a small factory, surely someone will be there. He tugs on the heavy metal door handle to open it. "Hello? Anyone here?" He approaches the single counter and leans against it.

The room is simple, just a counter separating the space. Beyond the counter is a phone and a bunch of papers scattered across the floor. A single door seems to lead to the factory. With his stomach aching and feet sore, he doesn't have much patience. He cracks open the door and again quietly asks, "Hello?"

He hears rustling in the distance but can't see anything due to barely any light and towers of boxes. He walks along the wall and discerns voices. He approaches a tall tower of boxes, but before he can turn the corner, he hears a man yell, "Shut the hell up."

His heart jumps into his throat and pounds in his chest. He slowly peeks around the corner. To his surprise, he sees three men holding guns, standing next to a large wood table. In front of them are four men and a woman kneeling on the factory's cold, filthy floor. A door opens behind the men.

*****

"Hey, Rook. Ya made it. What the hell took ya so long? You tuggin' one out?"

Jake approaches the scene. "Holy shit, Vern. What do we have here? You caught 'em?"

"You idiot. Look over there at that table." Vern points to a wood table separating them from their kneeling guests.

Jake walks toward a pile of cash and two boxes filled with tightly wrapped bricks of something. He immediately presumes it's drugs. He faces Vern. "I thought we got reports about thefts in the area?"

"Well, we got a tip, alright—a tip that's gonna let me retire a bit earlier than expected, and you know what? These five are the thieves. They're trying to move my money."

Jake watches the five thieves' faces whiten with fear, and blood drips from one man's ear. "Alright, well, let's cuff 'em and get outta here."

"Well, Rook, it's not gonna be that simple. You see, being Christmas and all, I figure we should get our gifts a little early."

"Tommy, Sam? What the hell is going on here?" Jake asks.

Sam just stands with his usual blank stare.

Tommy grins. "Don't cha get it, Rook? We just made a big payday, and we were nice enough to let you in."

"So, you guys knew about this the whole time?"

Vern grabs Jake's shirt. "Damn, kid, grow up. Of course, we knew about this. That whole burglary thing was just a bunch of bullshit. This bust is staying off the record."

Jake places his hand over his forehead. "So ... what? We're just gonna let these criminals go? They'll tell someone. Before you know it, we'll have a drug boss and our own department up our asses. Stop this bullshit. Let's call this in and go home."

Vern saunters toward the five kneeling. "You know what, Rook? You're pretty damn smart. I mean, hell, all I wanted was a nice payday instead of the joke salary. We bust our ass every day, and what do we get? A divorce, empty bank accounts, and kids who resent us. Screw that shit. But you're right; we can't let these guys tell their boss."

Jake exhales. "Thank god, you're finally making some sense."

Vern points his gun at Jake. "You know what? Actually, I think I do want to let these guys go." He stands over the first man kneeling on the floor. "Hey, look at me. Look at me! You wanna be free, son?"

The man eyes him but remains silent. His body shakes, his fear too great.

"Dammit, son, I asked you a question. Do you wanna be free?"

He moves his lips to quietly whisper, "Yes."

Vern takes a deep breath. "You got it." He places the end of the barrel to the man's head and pulls the trigger.

The man falls to his side, motionless, blood pouring from his head.

The woman screams.

"My god," Jake yells, reaching for his gun.

"I don't think so," Sam says, with his pistol aimed at Jake. "I'll take that for now." Sam grabs Jake's gun.

Vern yells, "Tommy, you're up."

Tommy walks over. Pop! Pop!

Two more men fall over, their souls escaping their body.

Jake falls to his knees and puts his head in his hands.

Vern laughs. "Oh, stop being such a pussy. You're up."

"The hell I am. I'll never do it!"

"But you just did," Vern says, with a stern look and signals to Sam.

Sam tosses Jake's gun to Vern.

"Sorry, honey, life's a bitch."

The hot steel bullet pierces the woman between the eyes. Her body slumps but doesn't fall.

Vern takes one step, places his boot to her chest, and kicks her over. "There you go, Rook, your first cherry pop."

Without a word, Sam meanders over, places the barrel atop the last man's head, pointing to the floor. He pulls the trigger, sending the bullet from the skull straight through his body. Sam looks up and moans in self-gratification.

Jake is frozen with shock.

"Alright, let's get out of here. Grab the shit. Let's go." Vern holsters his gun.

Jake notices it's not the police-issued pistol. Sam and Tommy have different ones too.

"Well, unless you want life in prison for murdering that pretty little thing, I suggest you keep your mouth shut and take your due."

Jake stays motionless and silent.

The guys bag up everything.

*****

The on-looking delivery man breaks from his trance. He turns his shaking body to escape, but his knee skims a stack of boxes. Like a slow-motion scene in a movie, the tower leans. He knows he can't stop it, so he runs. A second later, the tower crashes to the floor.

The men stop and notice a man run from the room.

Vern yells, "Stop him, Tommy."

Tommy runs around the maze of boxes, pushes through the doorway, and reaches the front lobby. He slams open the front door and stops at the sidewalk curb, frantically scanning the dim street. The trail is gone; the man could have gone in any direction. "Shit!" Tommy turns and returns through the lobby toward the front desk.

Well, what do we have here? Tommy approaches the counter and finds the shipping slip for the package, then returns to the slaughter to find the room deathly quiet. The bodies are hunched together, and the blood has pooled so much that a thin stream moves down the pitch of the floor for a small drain.

Vern angrily yells, "Where's he at?"

"He got away, but I found this." Tommy hands the slip to Vern.

With a quick glance, Vern smirks in relief. "Alright, saddle up, boys. Let's go, Rook. It's all over now, and just think, you have no choice but to make some money tonight."

"So, we clean, boss?" Tommy asks.

"C'mon, boy. 'Course it's all good. These fine entrepreneurs came here to make a trade. Whoever they were dealing with figured they should just keep it all. They took care of 'em and took off."

Tommy eyes Jake. "See, kid. It's all good. We rich, and we just had some good ole goddamn fun!"

Vern bends down next to woman, examining the area, and picks up something. "Yup, straight through. We wouldn't want this bullet laying around, now, would we, Jake? I'll just hold onto this for safekeeping." Vern gives a little wink and approaches him.

Jake surveys the scene, knowing he must play along. "Well, you boys sure do have some fucked up fun."

"Ahh-ha-ha. That's the spirit, boy. We'll make a cop of you yet." Vern puts his arm around Jake. "You just play nice, and everything will be all right, and maybe when the captain retires and I take over, you can run your own shit. Alright, like I said, let's get the fuck out of here."

Moments later, the men drive away. Jake stares out the window as Christmas signs pass by. "Merry Christmas my ass," he whispers.

*****

A stunned man hides in a corner alley, behind a trash bin, unsure he understands what he witnessed. He heads to his truck. A radio from inside a shop is still on; a faint sound travels to the streets. "Silent night, holy night, all is calm ..."

Chapter 2

"Good morning, sweetie. Wake up." Christine leans toward the master bed. "Megan made you a special breakfast."

"Hun, it's Saturday," Jake whispers in a raspy voice. "You have all day to nap, and your daughter made you a special daddy breakfast."

"Okay, okay." Jake sits upright and stretches. He goes to the closet to find his robe. He pulls it off the hanger and sees the shoebox he placed in the back corner nearly six months ago. It's filled with regret and remorse—stacked bills he refuses to use but doesn't really know what to do with. He shoves it farther back with his foot and wraps the soft robe around his body. "I'm coming, Megs. What did you make for me?"

Jake descends the stairs and finds a scene from some comedy film. Flour and sugar cover the counters, eggs drip to the floor, and milk is spilled.

"I made you special firework pancakes." In the pan is a glob of mix, surrounded by little dots of dye-colored mix.

"Those look great, honey."

"Happy Fourth of July, Daddy," Megan says with a smile.

"You too, baby. Start getting cleaned up for the party later, okay? I'll eat these up."

Megan runs from the room.

Jake pulls a piece of the pancake from the pan and eats it. "Woo-wee, I think she forgot something," he says, laughing.

Christine smiles. "She's just like her daddy, gets all excited and forgets what she's doin'." The phone rings, and Christine answers it. "Hello? Of course, he's right here. One sec." She hands the phone to Jake.

She can hear the voice from the phone across the room. "Hey, Jake. Sorry to call you, but we need you to come in. We're light over here and need you. It'll only be a couple hours."

Jake sighs. "Alright, Vern. I'm on my way." He hangs up and eyes his wife. "I gotta go in for a few. I'll be back for the party. Just call the station if you need anything." He leans over and kisses his frustrated wife. He grabs the milk jar and takes a big swig, inspecting his robe. "Well, I can't go like this. Though I'm sure the boys would love it."

Jake goes to his room to get dressed.

*****

As he arrives at the station, Jake notices the extremely bare parking lot. Entering the building, he sees Vern, Sam, and Tommy huddling around Vern's desk. A secretary in the front dispatches calls, and another lady in back files some papers.

"Where's everybody?"

"Oh, some are home, and some out on calls," Vern replies.

"Well, why'd you call me in? It looks like you three have things covered."

Vern stands up. "We just got back. Thought we could use another body if the town's party got outta hand."

Jake nods and sits at his desk. He's pissed they called him in and really doesn't have much to do, but to avoid the guys, he pretends to review some cases.

An hour passes, and the station remained absolutely silent.

Vern approaches Jake. "Hey, let's take a ride around town, see if anything's going on."

"How about you just let me go home? This place is dead."

"I'll tell you what. We check out some things for about an hour, then we come back, and you can take off. Sound good?"

Knowing that's probably the best offer he'll get, Jake agrees. He puts away his things and meets Vern outside by the car. As he closes in, he notices Sam and Tommy are already in it.

"Vern, you really need all of us to go?"

"Well, Rook, it wouldn't be fair if I let you go home and make these guys sit around, now, would it?"

Jake doesn't answer. He opens the back door, plops in, and slams it behind him. They know he doesn't like them, and they don't like him. Ever since the incident, Jake hasn't really said a word to them. He minds his business and hopes to get by. They take off down the road, leaving the station essentially empty.

Chapter 3

At a ranch, about forty miles from town, a family celebrates the Fourth of July by having a nice picnic. Mark grills meat for the family; steaks and burgers are the main course. He flips a burger, and he takes another sip of his fresh, cold beer.

His brother-in-law Wyatt stands with him, chatting about everything under the sun. "Oh, hey, congratulations on the raise, Mark. I guess you can afford those steaks now."

"Yeah, it's been a long time coming. I'm just glad we can save a little now." Mark grins and resumes grilling.

Inside, Mark's wife, Carol, puts together the pasta salad, and her sister Beth assists. They would much rather be inside anyway; the heat is a roaring ninety-eight degrees. The fan in the kitchen is on high, and the cold iced tea helps them stay cool. Carol watches Grandma rock the baby outside in the shade to keep the baby as cool as possible. They probably won't be out too much longer. Carol adds the salad toppings as her sister gossips.

Way in the back, past the small cornfield and toward the edge of the woods, the children play hide-and-seek. Sonny is "it;" he's Mark and Carol's first child and now the oldest, with the arrival of the baby last year. His cousins, two girls and one boy, are hiding. They only have one hundred seconds, so they must be quick. Sonny begins, "One hundred, ninety-nine, ninety-eight …"

*****

Jake and the men drive down an old dirt road in the middle of nowhere.

"Where are we going?" Jake asks.

Vern replies, "It ain't too far. Just wanna check on a few things. We'll be back before ya know it."

Tommy leans over the seat and turns up the radio. "Jumpin' Jack Flash. Whoo, I love this song!" Tommy sings the chorus as they continue deeper off the beaten path.

All Jake can think of is popping that first beer and hanging with his beautiful family.

*****

"Fifty, forty-nine, forty-eight …"

Mark slices the steak to check if it's that perfect medium rare. "Hey, babe! About five minutes!"

"Thirty-six, thirty-five, thirty-four …"

Grandma sees the children come through the cornfield to scope out their spots near the house. The little boy slides under the picnic table and puts his finger over his mouth at Grandma. The two girls hide together behind a bush near the back door. They can't help but giggle.

"Twenty, nineteen, eighteen ..."

*****

The dark car with Jake and the men turn left onto a narrow driveway and continue slowly.

*****

"Ten, nine, eight, seven ... Six, five, try to stay alive. Four, just three counts more. Three, you better hide from me. Two, I'm coming for you. One, time to have some fun!" Sonny steps from the huge oak tree to search the woods. It's hot, but a breeze blows through the leaves. He heads toward the cornfield and investigates every log and tree along the way, hoping they're somewhere in the wooded area; he hates going into the cornfield. After a few moments, he guesses they must have gone in there and steps into the field. "Where are you?"

*****

The car pulls up to a quiet and seemingly vacant house, yet a truck and a station wagon are parked by the garage. Vern parks the car and gets out. Tommy and Sam jump out and head to the trunk.

Jake, confused, exits the car and looks around. Nothing makes sense, and he doesn't have a good feeling about it. Why did Vern call him in the first place? Why wasn't anyone at the station? Why were these four together? "Alright, Vern, what are you up to. Where are we?"

Vern ignores Jake and unlocks the trunk.

Tommy nudges passed Jake to extract a shotgun from the trunk. Something doesn't look right though; the barrel is cut short, and the paint and markings are stripped.

Sam retrieves a large rifle and looks down the barrel.

Vern grabs another shotgun. He unholsters his pistol and sets it in the back to grab a .44 instead.

Jake reaches to slam down the trunk, but Sam grabs Jake's shirt. "You better just be still, boy."

Jake's face turns beet red. In a slow, quiet voice, he tries to speak. "Vern, what are you about to do?"

Vern glares deep into his eyes. "Sorry. Sometimes we ain't got a choice."

"What? What times? What choices?" Jake places his head on his arm that rests over the car. The confusion and uncertain fear swirls through his head.

Vern and Tommy approach the side of the house, while Sam heads to the porch and slowly enters. As he canvases the rooms, he sees family pictures lining the walls and hallway. The living room walls are bright blue, with flower patterns. He enters the hallway connecting the living room to the kitchen. He grabs a letter opener laying on top a pile of ripped envelopes from a nightstand.

Outside, Vern and Tommy cut the corner of the house.

Mark turns from hearing the footsteps. His eyes widen, and he stumbles backward into the grill, dropping the spatula, "Wait. Just hold on!"

"How you doin'? It's Mark, right?" Vern asks with a satisfying look.

Mark raises his hands outward. "I didn't say a thing. I don't know anything. Please!"

*****

Inside the kitchen, not hearing the commotion, the women continue preparing.

Sam, nearly in the kitchen, takes one quiet step at a time toward the two, then stops directly behind Beth.

Beth reaches for a towel to dry her hands but feels a sharp pain and extreme burn slide across her throat. As she grabs her neck, warm blood runs through the space between her fingers.

Sam quickly slides toward Carol. As she turns, Sam covers her mouth with his left hand and plunges the knife into her side. He retracts it once, then forced it in again.

Beth's hand runs across the counter for a pointless cure. She tries to speak but only chokes more. Blood gurgles as she exhales. She whips her head toward Carol, her eyes wide with panic.

Sam holds Carol tight as her wound worsens. Carol watches her sister collapse as her body tingles and weakens, becoming numb, and slides down Sam's chest. Her eyes flutter shut as she goes to sleep.

Sam releases, and she slides to the floor, where her head lands on Beth's stomach. The room is quiet. Sam walks toward the back and slams the knife through an onion resting on a cutting board. The knife sticks straight up, while a chunk of red onion slides across the counter.

*****

"Well, Mark, you shouldn't have been so nosey. I mean, why the hell were you working so late anyway?" Vern tilts his head.

"Hey, do we have a problem here?" Mark's brother-in-law asks, stepping alongside Mark.

"Ahh, boy, yes there's a problem. For you!" Vern says as an explosion sounds and echoes through the woods. The shotgun unloaded pellets straight into Wyatt's chest, splattering blood over Mark and the side of the house.

"Carol, run," Mark screams.

The back door opens, and Sam walks out.

Mark notices red spots on Sam's shirt and more on his hand. Mark falls to his knees, head buried into his lap.

Jake, hearing the shotgun blast, heads toward the back.

The two girls behind the bush try hard to stay quiet, but one whimpers.

Mark spies the bush, knowing everyone heard them. "Run, girls!" Mark jumps up, trying to stop Vern.

Vern quickly takes the butt of the gun and strikes Mark's head, taking him to the ground. Vern pumps the shotgun, turns, and aims for the girls running side by side toward the cornfield. He pulls the trigger and hits both from the back with one spread.

Jake turns the corner and sees the girls tumble over each other, like two rabbits in a field.

The baby cries in the background.

Mark rolls over, trying to get up.

Vern places his boot on his back.

Jake unholsters his gun and points it at Vern. "Not again. I won't let this happen all over again."

Vern smirks. "Let it happen? This was your idea. I mean, that's why you came to work on your day off, right? Hell, you wrangled all us up. Right, Sam?"

"Mm-hmm, that's right."

"Hey, Rook!" Tommy leans over the picnic table and grabs the boy trying to stay hidden. Tommy pulls the boy to stand him upright. He runs his fingers through the boy's hair.

Jake glares at Tommy. "He's just a boy. Have you no mercy?"

Tommy moves his hand to the boy's shoulder. "I hope God does."

Jake tightly shuts his eyes. His body jolts when the shot fires. A vibration moves through his core as a thud hits the ground.

All is silent, only the whimpers of an old lady and the crying of a baby. Mark's face is planted into the ground, motionless, knowing his time here is over.

Jake hears a faint rustle in the distance and sees Sonny on the ground through the thick stalk.

Vern yells, "Finish up. The party's over!"

Jake pushes himself off the ground with all he's got. He rushes Vern and tackles him to the dirt. The two wrestle, trying to get atop the other. Jake reaches his hand around Vern's neck, thumbs in the center of Vern's throat. He presses with all his might. Vern's eyes pop out, and tears roll to the side of his face. He squeezes harder.

Whack!

Daylight darkens for a second. Pain rushes to Jake's head. He looks up, dazed, at Sam standing over him, holding a rock.

Vern coughs as he rises, then kicks Jake's ribs. "You stupid little shit! Alright, finish up and let's go!" Vern approaches Mark and fires a shot to his skull.

Tommy turns, staring into Grandma's eyes, as the baby cries.

Grandma grits her teeth. "You'll be taken care of in Hell!"

Tommy looks at the trees; only the sound of a single baby crying is audible. The leaves on the branches are full and vibrant, squirrels jump from branches, and birds sit, resting. Large clouds forming familiar shapes cover the blue sky. The smell of sweet barbeque fills the air.

Boom!

Birds burst skyward from the trees, echoing their sound of flapping wings, then silence.

The men approach Jake. "It's all over, princess. Now get your ass to the car."

Jake quickly points his gun at Vern.

Vern laughs. "You gonna shoot me now? A little too late, don't cha think? Ha-ha. And what? You gonna add a cop to your count list?"

Jake yells, "I'll kill you all and myself, if I have to."

Tommy points his finger. "You ain't got a chance to kill all of us. I'll be sure to put you down. When I'm finished wit you,

I'll visit your ole lady and that little bitch of yours. Yeah, I'll treat 'em real nice!"

Jake rages, "Get out of here, you pieces of shit!"

Vern turns away. "A'ight, boys. Let's go. He can find his own way home. He ain't gonna say shit. He knows what we're capable of."

As the men walk toward the car, Jake can't help but wonder why; why him? He bends over and vomits on the grass. His heart pounds a thousand beats a minute. He took a big chance pulling that gun on Vern. He just knew he had to get them away—away from the last living soul of this slaughtered family.

He approaches Sonny in the field. His body is fire hot, shaken to the core. Jake tries talking to him, but his eyes fixate on the gruesome scene. Jake knows he's in extreme shock and that it might take a while to snap him from it. He picks up the boy and walks him into the house. He lays him on a couch and places a cold cloth over his head, then grabs the phone. "This is Officer Keller."

Chapter 4

A year later, on a warm summer evening, Jake and Christine are sleeping in bed. Jake has been having terrible dreams ever since the massacre and needs help to sleep. He tosses and turns as mumbled words escape his mouth.

Christine wakes, as she does many nights. "Honey, honey, it's okay. It's just a nightmare." She shakes him until he violently comes to.

He stares at the ceiling, trying to piece the scattered dream.

Christine rolls over, like routine, and tries to fall back asleep.

Jake takes a deep breath and pulls his cover to the side. He slides into his slippers and heads for downstairs. He opens Megan's door. She's fast asleep, holding her little elephant. For a moment, Jake forgets everything and smiles.

After a quick stop from the fridge, he plops onto his couch, holding a cold beer. The evening light brightens as the TV turns on and sets in. "Tonight, we look back at the greatest tragedy in Littleton, Alabama." The weathered anchorman reports, "It's been one year since the Littleton Massacre, but the memory still breaks the hearts of the community. Deputy Sam Kersh awaits his death penalty, and Tommy Ginn has begun his life sentence without parole in a maximum-security prison upstate. The DA awarded Ginn a plea bargain for testifying and bringing light to a murder investigation that had remained unsolved. With part of the deal, Ginn also cleared Jake Keller, stating the real killers had manipulated him and put him in duress the entire time, and he had no part of any killing. Sergeant Vern Maxwell's suicide had negated bringing him to trial. Officer Jake Keller courageously brought the men to justice after revealing a surviving family member who witnessed what some have called, The Barbeque Slaughter. Now this very troubled young boy spends his days at the Prairie Hill facility, an institution for the emotionally damaged. His treatment—"

Jake turns off the TV and leans back. He takes another sip and slowly falls asleep.

*****

The following day, the Fourth of July, is bright and sunny, with the temperature hitting a high of ninety degrees. While most people celebrate America's independence, the day haunts Jake. He pulls up to a clean, colorful facility, with large green bushes and flowers that decorate the lawn. As he approaches the front desk, workers and nurses welcome him with good morning nods and smiles.

A doctor notices him at the front and welcomes him back. "Good morning, Deputy. He just woke up a bit ago. Go ahead."

Jake walks the hallway and peeks into each room. He doesn't want to pry, but the sight of these poor confused people piques his natural interest. With every patient, he clenches his lips and shows his sympathy. He peers into Sonny's room at the boy, staring at the ceiling. Although Sonny is awake, it looks like he's sleeping with his eyes open. The room is very simple—a bed and a table with a lamp. The walls are off-white, and a large wooden cross hangs in the center of one.

Jake enters. "Hey, Sonny. How are you? I brought you something." He reaches out to hand Sonny a toy car.

Sonny blinks but doesn't show much emotion.

"Okay, I'll just set it over here for now." Jake sits on the corner of the bed. "You know, I'm …" He sniffles and wipes his face. "I'm so sorry, Sonny. I should have done more. I should have stopped it." Jake grabs Sonny's hand and gently squeezes. "Please forgive me. Please. I hope you can one day forgive me."

As he hangs his head, the doctor steps in. "I'm sorry to interrupt."

"It's okay. How's he doing?"

"Well, some days are better than others, and today doesn't seem to be one of the good ones. You know, since the day you brought him here, he has worsened. I mean, at least, a year ago, he would move around more and have small conversations, but lately he mainly just nods, maybe says yes or no, and repeats a rhyme over and over."

Jake furrows his brows. "Rhyme? What rhyme?"

"I don't know. He counts down and says something like, 'Five, something alive. Four,' umm, 'three things more. Two, he's coming for you, and one, he's gonna have some fun.' I don't know; it's something like that."

"Sonny? You wanna sing the song?" Jake asks.

Sonny continues to stare.

"Okay. It's okay. Well, Doc, I don't know either, but I wouldn't be surprised with anything after seeing what this kid witnessed."

"Yeah, I suppose you're right. Alrighty then, sir, you have yourself a nice Fourth. I got to get back to the rest of our friends." He raises his hand and doffs his imaginary hat, like a true cowboy.

Jake nods in return, regards Sonny one last time, and sighs. He pushes himself off the bed and straightens his shirt.

As he walks to the door, a voice behind whispers, "Five, try to stay alive. Four, just three counts more. Three, you better hide from me. Two, I'm coming for you. One, time to have some fun."

The hair on Jake's neck rises as he spins around. "Sonny, what was that? Sonny? Sonny?" It's like the boy was a radio, spitting sound from a lifeless box. After a few moments of trying to communicate, Jake says goodbye and leaves the room.

The rhyme plays repeatedly in his head all the way home. He knew he'd heard it before, but where? From whom? The car pulls up the driveway, and before it can completely stop, the memory of the rhyme hits him. He remembers Megan once singing a slightly different version while playing tag or hide-and-seek. He wonders if Sonny was playing a game before he saw the massacre. It must be stuck in his mind or subconscious. The thought gives him a painfully sour stomach. He can't help but feel he's to blame.

His self-disgust shows vividly on his face during supper.

Christine knows why he seems so sad and decides to wait to address it after dinner. A few hours later, Christine goes into the bedroom and finds Jake already there. He lays on his side, facing away. Christine lays down, facing up, and places her hand on him. "I know nothing anyone can ever say or do will ever make what happened okay. You need to know and believe that you are a good man—a great man. You have a family who loves you so much and will be by your side forever. It'll get better. I swear it. I love you so much." Christine slides her hand down and turns over.

Jake's eyes close, pushing a stream of tears to his pillow.

Chapter 5

Twenty years have passed, and a forty-six-year-old wakes in his bed, one side perfectly made. He traverses the hallway but stops at a cracked door and pushes it open. A skeleton of a room resides; a sheet and a single pillow cover a bed in the center. The dresser is empty, and a frame holds a picture of memories long lost. Megan's Room remains painted on the wall over the closet door. He slowly pulls the door shut, then pauses. The aroma of coffee breaks his trance, and he heads to the kitchen.

After a few bites of toast and a final drink, he leaves for work. The police station is very bright and clean. Many renovations have occurred over the past twenty years. When Jake walks through the station, everyone addresses him. He should have been in charge by now. His good friend Deputy Maison Stone gives him a smirk.

"I see you turned down the promotion again."

"And I will again and again and again," Jake says with a laugh. "I love what I do and don't want to get caught sitting behind a desk. Plus, I wouldn't get all this time off. You saw the bass I snagged last week. A fish like that doesn't get hooked by chance"

Maison shakes his head. "Yeah, yeah, so you gonna see him today? I mean, you haven't missed in twenty years. Don't know why I even asked. I gotta say, I admire what you do."

Jake's expression becomes serious. "Well, that boy deserved a much better life than this. Everything was stolen from him. Hell, in a way, they took both our families from us."

"You're just passionate."

Jake sighs. "I should have been passionate with more than just my work. One day I'll have my family back, and so will he. Hey, shouldn't you be out there patrolling? You know someone's gonna blow their finger off this year. Damn drunk fools."

The two laugh and go their way. Jake accomplishes a few tasks and prepares to take off for a few days.

*****

Later that day, Jake pulls up to Prairie Hills. The facility looks much older now. The paint has chipped off the wood posts, and the front sign has all but rusted through. The place is still functional, however, with nearly twenty-five patients and twelve staff members.

Jake enters the room.

Sonny lays on his side, looking at the wall. His body takes up the whole bed now, and his legs hang off the end.

The now weathered doctor enters. "Good afternoon, fine sir. How have you been?"

"Oh, the same as last time, living day to day."

"Well, I have some good and bad news. The bad news is, Sonny remains uncommunicative for the most part. As you know, it slowly worsened over the years, and I feel it has hit its peak. However, what remains is his random meaningless words and childlike rhymes. This last year, and especially the last few months, have been quite interesting. He now responds to internal emotions."

Jake pursed his lips. "What exactly do you mean? He's responding to people and talking?"

"No, no. Again, he doesn't talk or communicate, but when a patient becomes unorderly or when someone yells or throws things, Sonny shakes and becomes angered. Last week, we found his room destroyed. He was in the corner, hitting his head against the wall. This was right after we had to subdue a violent patient. We also found a dead rat under his bed, but it wasn't just dead; its body was flattened to the ground."

Jake's eyes widen. "Oh my god! Well, what in the hell could be the good news?"

"As I said, this only happens when he gets frightened or responds to another's anger. We've been conducting an experiment with him. We have a supply hut about five miles from here. We keep all our extra supplies there because we just don't have enough room or money to expand. Ritchie has been taking Sonny for trips once a week to the hut, to help bring supplies back."

"Really? I know Ritchie and the boy have always had a good bond. How's that working?"

"The good news is, he has been great with it. He still doesn't talk, but he listens to Ritchie's requests and follows. It's quite amazing. Ritchie has also found him near the pond there, admiring the scenery. Now, we didn't tell you about this 'cuz we wanted to try it out first. You understand, right?"

"No, that's great. I'm so happy to hear he enjoys getting out. Oh, that's wonderful news. Just please let me know if anything goes wrong or if those violent episodes get worse."

"Of course, Jake, of course."

A man enters the room, as if on cue.

"Speaking of the devil," Jake says, grinning. "I hear you've been taking really good care of my boy here. I really appreciate it. So, how's the family, Ritchie?"

"Can't complain. Everyone's healthy and doing well. And yours? Oh god, I'm sorry, Jake. Just habit, you know?"

"Yeah, I know. Anyway, I'm glad to hear Sonny's helping with supplies."

"This place is packed to the max. I mean, the old supply room has two patients occupying it right now. In reality, we have all the stuff we need. Just keep a few odd items out there or old unused things. Sometimes I don't even need to go there, but I think someone enjoys it." Ritchie winks.

"Alright, gentlemen. It seems you have it all under control. I want you to know it means a lot to me. Well, I'm off. You can bet there will be enough drunks to handle tonight." Jake leaves the room and heads out.

Ritchie places his hand on Sonny's shoulder. "Alright, let's go for that drive."

*****

Ritchie and Sonny ride down a lonely road in an old Ford pickup. After about five miles, Ritchie turns onto an unmarked dirt road. The entire way down, Sonny stares outside, but his eyes don't move. Dense woods, appearing uncharted, surround the last stretch of road. They finally see the storage hut—a medium-size shack that looks like a onetime cozy little home. Behind is a lake that resembles a large pond, surrounded with wild weeds and tall grass. The view is pretty, with frogs croaking and birds singing their tunes. The sound forms music and fills the empty air.

Ritchie opens the door and tells Sonny to go ahead.

Sonny shuffles to a bench, sits, and stares into the water.

Ritchie enters the shack. The structure houses old wheelchairs with broken spokes and dusty wooden chairs and desks, along with a noticeably newer shelving unit containing bandages, alcohol, syringes, and most common hospital supplies. A cabinet next to it holds a moderate number of canned goods, peanut butter, and other nonperishables. Dirty nurse uniforms and doctor robes lay in the corner, as well as a large amount of soiled, ripped patient garments.

Ritchie grabs the last of the items and looks out the single dark pane window. He pans left to the pond and sees an empty bench. "Sonny?" He turns toward the door and approaches the opening. With his arms filled with things, he gets to the doorway.

Sonny turns the corner.

"Ah, my god boy. You scared the shit out of me! Go grab the alcohol for me. It's the clear bottle on the shelf over there." Ritchie throws the supplies into the truck bed and hops inside.

Sonny takes the bottle and scans the shelves before turning to sit in the truck.

"Oh, I almost forgot." Ritchie jumps from the truck and locks the door. "Hell, it ain't like anyone comes out here anyway. Ain't that right, boy? It's our little paradise." Ritchie laughs as he hops back into the truck and heads out.

On the way to the hospital, Ritchie looks at Sonny, who's gazing out the window. "You know, Sonny, you're a great person. I want you to know that. You'll always be my friend, and one day, one day you'll have your family back."

Sonny's eyes twitch for a moment, then resume their dead gaze.

Chapter 6

That night, around 11:30 p.m., the hospital remains quiet. A security guard sits at the front desk, while three nurses make their rounds. In the break room, two janitors sit, talking about nothing, trying to waste time.

"Well, I guess I better start cleaning that back room," one of the men says, while placing a mouth guard on his face. "Too damn dirty back there."

The other man laughs. "You look cute, honey."

The masked man glances over his shoulder. "You wish." He chuckles and leaves.

The janitor still in the room stands and stretches. He takes a huge draw from his cigarette and strikes it across his jeans, red ash falling to the tiled floor. He steps on the ash and drinks from his Coke. He flips the cigarette butt into the trash and silences the radio. As he leaves, he pushes the indented seat under the desk covered with paper and trash. The door shuts behind him.

Ritchie twirls his keys while traversing the hallways, peeking into each room. He turns left down the next hallway and continues to the end, where two rooms sit on each side. On the left sleeps an old man with his sheet barely covering his legs. Ritchie looks through the right-side door window and views Sonny awake, eyes fixated. Ritchie heads back and passes a nurse who gives him a smile. He returns the gesture and checks the clock—12:12.

The rear of the facility is dark and quiet, a distinct difference from the front of the building. It seems those forgotten are roomed farther back. At the front of the building, a set of double doors separate the office from the patients' rooms. The nurse's smile remains as she opens her binder to record the night's data. Her pen clicks, and she writes.

Boom!

Lights flicker, and ceiling tile particles fall into her hair. She runs toward the offices and catches a janitor only steps ahead. As they turn to enter the adjacent hallway, they see a black cloud of smoke and an orange light from the roaring flames. The janitor's heart sinks. Within seconds he realizes the cigarette butt must have still been hot. The trash fire has spread through the room, igniting the oxygen tank kept in the corner.

The nurse screams, "Get them out! Get them all out!" She sees Ritchie come up behind. "We only have two keys. We must hurry."

The nurse and Ritchie scramble down the hallways, trying to free the patients from their soon-to-be-locked oven. Those in the office have already fled, blocked from the rest of the building. Flames ascend, consuming the surrounding oxygen and gaining energy. Gas lines throughout the facility have ignited. When they realize they can't save them all, an emergency door seems to be the last clear way out.

Screams, yells, and cries immerse into the smoky, hot air. Fire is nearly everywhere now. A man burns alive, scratching and clawing at the window. A woman is on her knees, grasping a rosary wrapped around her hands, praying and welcoming her creator to save her from the choking smoke and skin-melting heat. The nurse and Ritchie have opened almost half of the rooms. People panic and are on their own to survive. Some have reached the emergency room, some to the double doors to find themselves trapped.

With little time left, Richie peers down the narrow dark hallway to the end; flames lick both sides of the walls, and ceiling tiles have fallen. He runs through the ash and smoke to Sonny's room. He glances left to see the old man pounding on the door, but he only has time for one. He fumbles with the keys and jars open the door to Sonny standing there.

"Run! Get the hell out," Ritchie yells.

Sonny twitches, as to wake from a spell, and hustles down the hallway, feeling the screams pass through his body, like a hook piercing a nightcrawler. He can't help but remember his family's screams from twenty-one years ago. His steps are blunt, and he moves zombielike. He homes into the eyes of a young lady who has lost most of the skin on her face, just a dripping goo splatting to the floor. Everywhere he looks is pure agony.

Visualizations of the baby and the grandma's murder creep through his brain. He sees the bloody bricks and his father pleading for Vern not to hurt his family. He remembers the warmth of his mother's love and the pain of separation, tearing like a wet tongue frozen to metal—a long-lasting pain that never diminishes.

As a wood beam falls, Sonny snaps from his mind-numbing torture and turns back. He spots Ritchie laying on the floor, with one arm reached out. His legs are caught under a fallen doorframe. He appears lifeless from lack of oxygen. Sonny runs to him, grabs his arm, and drags him from the wreckage. Fire catches Ritchie's pants legs and trails up like a path set by gasoline.

Ritchie explodes with a fierce groan, his body covered in flames, which seem inextinguishable. "Go, go!"

Sonny falls backward, slipping from Ritchie's hand. Flames surround him too. Knowing he can no longer reach Ritchie, he looks to the ceiling and releases a mighty yell powered by the lifelong pain which has been festering ever since his family's massacre.

Outside, those who made it hold each other, flinching after every sound. Looking around, they easily see many are missing. Every passing minute steals the hope of ever seeing them again.

Chapter 7

The next morning, Jake pulls up to a crowded scene. Only a shell of the building stands, and a mist of smoke lingers in the air. Whimpering and sniffles surround the workers.

"Hey, Jake." Maison steps over and asks nervously, "How are you?"

In a remorseful, shaky haste, Jake responds, "I got here as soon as I heard. I can't believe it. I leave town for one night, and this shit happens. Where are the bodies?"

"Well, sir, most have burned, with everything else."

"Did you find Sonny?" Jake's voice cracks in anticipation.

Maison looks down. "Well, what I can tell you is that we have eight confirmed bodies, fourteen who made it out, and four are missing. Now, I'm sure they're all in there. We just need time. Plus, we can't even be sure who the eight bodies are. It'll take time to identify them. Sir, I'm really sorry, but it's over. You have to let him go."

Jake glares into Maison's eyes. "Find him!"

Before Maison knows it, Jake is already in his car. Pebbles fly across the road from tires gripping into the ground, and the smell of burned rubber lingers in the air.

*****

A week has passed.

"Hey, boss, you look like shit. You okay?" Maison asks Jake.

"Fine. Just haven't slept in a week."

"Sir, I know we couldn't confirm some of the bodies, but you gotta let it go."

"Don't tell me what to do! Who the hell do you think you are, dammit?" Jake pounds his fist on the desk.

"Whoa, hey. I—"

"Ahh, forget it. My head is killing me. I'm sorry. I'm just tired." He sighs.

Maison takes a deep breath. "Listen. I have to go to Perry Street. Mrs. Webster is missing. She's been fighting dementia for years now. Sure hope her family or I can find her soon before something happens. Just, just try to get some sleep." Maison leaves, slowly shutting the door behind him.

Jake leans backward, his head resting on the cushion of the seatback. The rough fabric scratches his neck and tugs his neck hair every time he settles in. As the sounds surrounding him blend and drown out, he dozes off. His mind races, forcing him into restless sleep. As dreams develop, his face clenches, and sweat collects on his forehead.

A dark grim world opens, flames rising high all around—a scene from Hell. His regrets of the past come forth. Visions of Sonny's family emerge, bloody faces everywhere. His old police mates laugh hysterically, proud of their sinister work, and a little boy crouches on his knees, crying. Jake sees the back of his wife walking out the front door and his daughter playing catch with her new dad. All these visions swirl in and out of another. The heat warms his body, and the flickering light dances the shadows behind each figure.

Voices echo in his head—Mrs. Webster and Maison. The voices louden, and the figures in his head diminish. As they grow louder, his heart races, and with an electrifying jolt, he wakes.

"Hey, Jake! You all right? Looks like you just came from the showers."

Jake wipes the sweat from his head. "Yeah, I'm fine. Find out anything?"

Maison scratches his chin. "Nope. It's weird, though. The family said she hasn't left the house in months. Man, that disease is terrible." He shakes his head. "Why don't you go home? I have things under wraps here. I'll let you know if anything comes up. Just close your blinds and get some rest."

Jake hesitates, then nods. "Yeah, maybe you're right. That's probably a good idea. Make sure you call me if anything comes up. Got it?"

"Yes, sir. You know it. Now get outta here."

Jake heads for the door. "Okay, I'll talk to you later tonight."

Chapter 8

It's quiet. Light voices carry through the window from outside, stifled by a whirling ceiling fan above Jake, who's asleep in his bed. The room is humid. The sun has warmed the window and walls, creating sauna-like temperatures in the room.

Ringgg ... Ringgg ... Ringgg ...

Jake slowly turns over to pick up the phone and clears his throat. "Yeah?"

A frantic Maison blasts his ears. "Hey, where've you been? You gotta get over here, fast!"

Jake replies in deep confusion, "What? What do you mean? What's going on?"

"You didn't come in yesterday, but you've been lookin' pretty shitty. Wanted to let you sleep."

"Wait, what? What day is it?"

"Friday."

"Oh, shit. I must have slept through the day."

"It doesn't matter. Just get over here. This shit's crazy. We're at 325 Maple Grove. Hurry!"

*****

Driving down the road, Jake can't help but wonder how he slept through an entire day. It only seemed like a few hours. He still feels exhausted. He figures it must be from oversleeping. He rocks his head back and forth, trying to stretch the kink in his neck and work out the soreness of his body. He feels like he worked on a construction site all night.

He sees the Maple Grove sign ahead and quickly remembers how startled Maison sounded and forgets about his ailments. The closer to his destination he gets, the more concerned he becomes. Emergency vehicles flood the street, and flashes of light flicker above camera lenses. The intrigued audience tries to avoid the yellow tape, which stretches across the property like the walls to a mouse maze

Jake leaves the car and approaches the front of the house. He sees Maison and nods.

Before Jake can speak, Maison begins, "Sir, I've never seen anything like this. We have a female, age twenty-nine, murdered by stab wounds to her chest and abdomen. The husband, thirty-eight-year-old Roger Simon, son Matt, and daughter Maddi are missing. Initial speculation is that it's a murder/kidnapping. We have an APB on the father. Jake, it's terrible in there. I've never seen so much blood."

Jake crosses his arms and shakes his head. "Okay, well, keep working here. I'll head to the station. Any new information on Mrs. Webster?"

Maison pauses. "Umm ... what? I mean, no. Sorry. I just can't get the images out of my head. When I came in, all I could see at first were a pair of legs sticking out from a doorway. Her flower dress was soaked in blood. When I turned to see the full body, I just, well ... But, umm, no. The family hasn't said anything further. We still have patrols looking around and checking churches in the area."

Jake purses his lips. "Keep it going and check back with me in a few hours."

"Will do."

Wind blows through the car as Jake travels down the road. He comes upon a small store and stops in. As he approaches the counter, he can tell the clerk already knows about the morning's tragedy.

"How ya doin'? Busy day, huh?"

"Yep. Not the morning I was expecting." Jake shows the clerk picture of Mrs. Webster. "Have you seen this woman?"

The clerk shakes his head. "Nope, but I know what you're talkin' about. A bunch of people have been searching the fields across the street. They came in here, too. I guess they didn't find anything."

Jake places his hand on his chin. "Hmm, well, thanks for your time." Jake walks through the front door and scans the field.

As he pans the horizon of corn stalks, he notices a farmhouse. A girl and her father shoot a basketball through a brown basket hung from a pole. His heart drops, and he imagines himself spending time with his daughter. He envisions her face, her smile, her laughter. Depression engulfs him, like a warm, wet blanket just dropped on his shoulders. Jake returns to his car and slowly steps in. With a big exhale, he drives off.

*****

After hours of patrolling around town, he heads to the station. When he arrives, he finds the building mostly abandoned. He decides it would be a good time to slip away and go home for some rest. He just doesn't feel right. His body is incredibly sore and still feels exhausted.

*****

At home, all is calm. Lights are dim. Jake grabs a glass of water and brings it into the bathroom so he can wash up for bed. The hot washcloth feels good on his face. He rubs vigorously, breaking away the dirt and filth layered on his skin. As he rings the discolored water from the cloth, he gazes into the mirror.

Ring, ring.

Jake snaps from his lost gaze and answers the phone. "Hello?"

"Hey, boss." Maison's voice travels through the speaker. "No sign of the family yet and still nothing on Webster. This day has been nothing but shit. We still think the dad took off with 'em, but who knows?"

"Alright. And yes, nothing but shit. I'll talk to you later. See ya in the morning."

Jake finally hits his mattress and slips his legs underneath the tightly tucked cool sheets. As his head nestles into the pillow, every inch of his body relaxes. He is so exhausted that his body almost feels like it's levitating above the fitted sheet. His eyes close, and consciousness of the world around disappears.

Moments later, he finds himself in a hazy world. A house is ahead; it looks familiar, but he's not sure. He climbs the porch steps, but a piece of yellow caution tape drags across his pants leg as he approaches the door. He slowly opens the door. The vision of the hallway inside is still blurry, but he discerns legs ascending the staircase. He turns his head and notices a man laying unconscious on the kitchen floor.

Another vision flashes of a woman running through the hallway in slow motion trying to turn, but her momentum carries her into the wall. A serrated blade lunges into her side. She takes another step, but her weakened body slides down the wall to the floor. Red smears across the off-white paint, like a demonic rainbow ending at her body. But this is no fairytale, only a horrific nightmare.

Two children dash from a closet and flee into their bedroom. A shadowy figure enters the room in chase—the same figure Jake saw climbing the staircase. The kids cling to each other in the corner. The man slowly reaches out.

A sharp gasp of air enters Jake's now-awakened lungs. "What the hell was that?" As he tries to remember all the pieces of the dream and gain composure, he spots the clock—5:47 a.m. He grabs the phone and dials. "Maison, hey, it's me. I need you to meet me at the station. Now." He hangs up without even waiting for a response, gathers himself, and leaves.

Chapter 9

Jake walks in and shouts, "I don't think it's a kidnapping. I can't really explain. I just have this feeling." In the background, a blinking light flashes on the side of a desk phone. Jake places his hand on his forehead. "Did you check that message?"

"What?" Maison eyes his desk. "Oh shit. I didn't see that." He slides his nameplate over and puts the receiver to his ear.

"Good morning. Forensics came back. We found Mr. Simon's blood in the house near the kitchen and another footprint, not the size of anyone in the family. We will be running more tests on the print. We have not found any indication of a struggle or of the children's blood. It seems to us that another person was in the home. We don't know if they were helping Mr. Simon, but from the blood found, we think that is less likely. If we get anything else, I'll let you know."

Maison sets the receiver on the hook switch phone and looks at Jake. "How'd you know? Forensics came back, and they think someone else was involved. They found Mr. Simon's blood in the house, too."

Jake shakes his head. "I don't know. I just had this crazy dream. It was so real. If all these people are dead, it's the biggest massacre since … well, you know." Jake gazes out the window. "Okay, Maison. Keep working on this, and I'll work on finding Mrs. Webster. I'm gonna head to their house to see if I can find some clue or something, anything. With this new information, we can't rule out anything. Who knows what happened to her."

The men leave the station and head their own way. Jake can't help feel exhausted and confused. He hasn't had enough sleep, and when he does, the nightmares are terrorizing. He's having a hard time knowing what's reality or a dream. He arrives at the Webster's and knocks three times, figuring everyone's out searching.

He turns the knob and enters. He looks around for a while and steps back toward the basement staircase. He descends slowly and reaches the base step. He stands motionless, scanning the room. He has an unsettling feeling but continues onward. Along the hallway, he sees a closet door ajar. Step after step, he lowers his hand toward his service weapon. His other hand slowly rises toward the edge of the door. With one quick jerk, he opens it and crouches, ready to attack.

He exhales when he realizes nothing is there; however, he notices a blanket, stained with a smudge, in the back corner. He picks it up and turns.

"Hey!" a man says from the doorway.

"Holy shit, Don," Jake shouts.

Mr. Webster steps backward. "I'm sorry, young man. I didn't mean to scare you, but what are you doing here?"

The pulse in Jake's neck slows. "I'm not sure. I just wanted to check on things, see if I could find any clues."

Mr. Webster furrows his brows. "Here? Inside the house? I don't understand."

Jake puts his hand on Don's shoulder. "I didn't mean to startle you. I'm just not leaving any stone unturned."

They ascend the stairs, into the kitchen.

"Can I get you anything? Soda or some water?" Don asks.

Jake spots a teakettle on the stove. On the counter sits a teacup and a half-ripped teabag wrapper. He lifts the kettle to find it's full of water. "Hey, Don, you making tea? It's pretty hot out."

"No, no. Margret was making some the night she left. She must have just forgotten. God, I don't know what I'm gonna do if I lose her."

Jake nods. "Don't worry, Don. We'll find her. I'll do whatever I can. I better get going."

Jake walks out the door to the porch. As he steps onto the pathway, he notices the front half of a large shoe print in the flowerbed. A warm, numb feeling engulfs him, and he envisions the old woman standing at the counter, opening her tea wrapper. A hand wraps around her face and covers her mouth. She stiffens and releases the tea wrapper, which falls to the surface.

Jake looks up from his daze. "Shit!" He runs to his car and slams the door.

*****

At the station, Deputy Maison is in the conference room, thanking the Beacon City Police Officers. "We really appreciate all your help."

Jake enters to see four pictures of the Simon family on the chalkboard. Deceased is written under Mrs. Simon, and Missing under the other three.

"Oh hey, Jake," Maison announces, "It's confirmed that another person was in the home. DNA also confirms Mr. Simon's blood."

"Yeah, well, you better add Mrs. Webster's picture, too."

"What?"

Jake crosses his arms. "I went to the house, and something's just not right."

Maison eyes the other men. "Okay, gentlemen. Let's take a break." The room clears. Maison sits on the desk's edge. "Jake, what's going on?"

Jake, too, sits. "Alright, so I went to the house. An open teabag was on the counter and a full kettle on the stove. I found a footprint in the flowerbed and dirt in the basement."

"Okay, so a normal scene at a home where people have been going in and out of."

"Man, I'm telling you!"

"Listen. We can't just go scaring people because of a hunch."

"Well, I had a hunch about the Simons."

"Yes, you did, and I was surprised, but we gotta be careful with this."

Jake releases a long exhale. "Whatever. All I'm saying is something's off."

Maison shakes his head in disbelief. "Okay, I'll put her on the board, but as missing."

Jake surveys the board, trying to wipe the sweat from his brow. He pans left to right at each picture. He shakes his head; something feels familiar, but he's having a hard time organizing his thoughts.

"Listen. You've been through a lot. These dreams you're having, little sleep, Sonny. You need a break or something. I know things are crazy right now, and we need all the hands we can get, but you are no good to us in this condition. You have to take a break."

Jake glares at him, wanting to object, but he knows Maison is right. He grabs his keys and heads toward the door.

*****

On the way home, Jake can't help but see the faces on the pictures tapped to the board. Images of Mrs. Webster and the Simon family swirl through his head. Before he knows it, he's sitting idle in his driveway. While he gazes out his car window, he thinks about his daughter and wife. He remembers the little picnic they had in the front yard and the lemonade stand Megan set up for passersby, sounds of laughter and play soothing his ears.

Another figure enters his mind—a young boy hiding in a field and turning into a young man. He recalls the fire and feels the guilt and remorse of his actions so many years ago. Suddenly, like an electrical shock, he comes to.

"No. No way," he murmurs.

He runs into the house and calls Maison—no answer—so he leaves a message. "Listen. I could be crazy, but I gotta talk to you first thing in the morning. I might have an idea of what's going on. God help me if I'm right!"

Jake enters his kitchen and grabs a small rocks glass from the cupboard and a bottle of Tennessee whiskey. He pours the liquid to the rim and takes a sip. He opens a closet door and grabs a flimsy box, coated with a layer of dust, sitting atop the shelf. He balances the glass on the lid as he brings it to the living room. He sits on his couch, places the glass on the table, opens the box, and removes a manila folder.

The tab reads: July 4th, 1979. He peruses the files and places the pictures across the table. He grabs the glass with a tight grip and swallows the remaining liquor. A large burning exhale escapes his mouth. Photos of death, blood, and remorse cover the tabletop. He leans backward and rests his head on the sofa cushion, closes his eyes, and slowly drifts away.

Chapter 10

The next morning, the warmth of the sun on Jake's face and the chirping of birds wakes him. Feeling that everything is good in the world, he stretches to fully wake. He glances at the empty glass on the table, immediately reminding him of his last thought before nodding off.

He shoves the pictures aside and grabs the phone to call his partner.

"Hello?" Maison answers.

"Hey, it's me. I called you last night."

"Yeah, I know. I just thought it would be best to leave you alone to get rest."

"Maison, I know this is gonna sound crazy, but I think Sonny's still alive!"

"What? Why?"

"I don't know. It's just that the people in these cases remind me of his family. I know it's crazy, just ... I don't know. It's like he's taking them back."

"Taking them back? Taking who back? Okay, say whatever you think is right. Why do we have a dead body? You can't take back the dead!"

"I don't know," Jake growls. "I'm going to the old hospital. I'll call you back later." He drops the receiver in haste and leaves it dangling over the table. As he hurries out the door, he hears Maison's voice through the speaker: "Jake. Jake! You have to stop this! You're starting to lose it!"

Out the car window, he sees trees and brush fly by. The painted lines of the road pass one by one underneath the car's front bumper. Jake slows the car. The Prairie Hills Hospital sign is in sight. He stops in front of the abandoned building. Nothing but lone standing walls and pieces of burned debris lay scattered over the facility's grounds. He presses the accelerator and pulls away. The hospital is faint in the rearview mirror as he continues onward.

He turns the wheel gently to the right, sliding across the loose gravel and spitting rocks as the tires spin, onto an old, dirt road—the same path Ritchie and Sonny would take on their trips, blanketed by trees and vegetation. The sky is hardly visible; only minor beams of light shine through.

Creatures stop in curiosity to the sound of the engine. Jake sees the old shed that would supply the economically busted hospital. He stops and takes a moment to enjoy the peace of nature. The pondwater is still, except for one jet stream splitting behind a bullfrog's swim. A cool, moist breeze travels through the trees, gently parting leaves from swaying limbs.

Jake approaches the shed and notices the door cracked open. With no lock in sight, he opens the door and inspects his surroundings, noticing a pile of old doctor and nurse scrubs spread across the floor, with a balled towel near the head of what looks like a makeshift bed. The shelves are messy with tipped-over bottles, bandages, and discarded medical equipment. He can't believe it, but this must be Sonny's new home. He feels sick when he thinks of the boy's tattered life and the monster they may have created. Jake leaves, trying not to disturb anything and to not give away his knowledge of the hideout.

On his way home, he calls Maison to check in. "Any news?"

"Nope, not yet, but it's a zoo here. How about you?"

"I've found some interesting things but nothing solid. I really think we need to realize that Sonny must be behind this. He was very unstable, and with all the mental issues he's had, plus the fact he's missing—"

"Listen, Jake. Right now is not a good time for you to be promoting this. The people around here are worried but not yet scared out of their minds. They would freak if they thought a killer was on the loose. Plus, they know about your history with him. I don't want the captain to pull you off the case. Go home. I can handle it here for now—"

"I'm not a fool or crazy! I'm telling you, Mrs. Webster is either dead or captive somewhere, and Sonny has something to do with it. This is bullshit!" He throws the phone across the dashboard and heads home.

When he enters, he sees files scattered on the table. He grabs them and violently whips them across the room. Pain rushes to his head, and he tucks his chin into his chest. He tries to press the sides of his skull, hoping to relieve the tension. He collapses to the couch and lays in the fetal position. The scratchy material rubs against his cheek. He lays motionless, his heart calming.

Chapter 11

On a beautiful street at dusk, a family prepares for the day's end with a barbeque. Tina and her friend Carrie sit in the back, drinking sweet tea. Tina's husband, John, mans the grill, advising his teenage son David how to cook the perfect steak. David's sexy sun-dressed girlfriend Mona plays in the sandbox with Carly, Carrie's little girl. While Mona digs her feet farther into the sand, she pushes Carrie's other baby daughter, Jessie, in a rocker.

*****

On the sidewalk out front, a man ambles past without expression or acknowledgment of the world around him, until he approaches the walkway to a simple colonial-style home and hears laughter and conversation in the back. He saunters to the front. The red wooden door is wide open, while the screen door is shut, letting the breeze travel through. The man opens the screen, and as he moves around the metal frame, a gust of wind blows an American flag hanging over the mailbox onto his cheek and gently falls away. He enters the home, and the screen shuts behind him. He finds a door leading to the basement and proceeds down.

*****

John, outside, thinks he heard a door shut and asks David if he heard anything.

He shakes his head. "No, but I can check." David walks through the house to the front, seeing the front door screen. He scans the street, shrugs, and turns to see a picture hanging on the wall that's been there for years—a vacation taken a long time ago at a waterpark. The family looks happy. After pausing for a moment, he gently closes the basement door that someone must have left open. "Nope, nothing, Dad. Hey, does anyone need anything while I'm in here?"

There's no answer.

*****

Out back, Carrie leans toward Tina. "Thank you so much for letting us stay the night. I can't wait to meet up with Bill in North Carolina, but the drive from Texas is just too much."

Tina smiles. "No problem. We love seeing you and the kids."

*****

Later that night, John gives blankets to Carrie for her and the kids. He shows her the den. David and his girlfriend have moved upstairs to his room to watch a movie. John opens the door to the master bedroom, revealing his wife wearing a light blue silk nightgown. He slides a glass of water across the nightstand and lays atop the bed. He smiles at Tina, kisses her goodnight, and turns off the reading lamp.

*****

At 3:17 a.m., the house is mostly dark. A glow comes from digital clocks around the kitchen, and moonlight shoots through the window.

Downstairs, deep breathing comes from a small room where the homeowners store old boxes and personal effects. The man sits with his head in his hands; the only movement is the arch of his back rising and falling with each breath. He slowly glances up. "Ten, nine, eight, seven, six, five, try to stay alive. Four, just three counts more. Three, better hide from me. Two, I'm coming for you. One, let's have some fun."

He slowly stands and walks through the door opening. With each step up the stairs, he feels the lives ahead. As if a resident for years, he travels through the home, avoiding obstructions, and finds another staircase that leads upward. Light creaking sounds while he ascends the wooden planks. The smooth, cool railing slides through his hand as he reaches its peak. A low-flickering light from under a bedroom door dimly illuminates the hallway, like a low-lit strobe slipping through the cracks of a haunted house.

He quickly pushes open the door to expose a muted TV playing The Wizard of Oz. The man approaches the dresser, dragging his finger across the mounted trophies and pictures. He stops to dust off a nameplate on a Little League baseball trophy. He grips the trophy's base and steps toward the bed, watching a beautiful goddess sleep, only wearing laced panties, and her legs wrapped over David.

David subconsciously feels a presence and awakens. "What the fu—?"

With tremendous force, the man bashes the trophy into the bridge of David's nose, caving in his face. He strikes one more time and turns the bloody trophy over in his hand. Before she can even scream, he stabs the goddess in the throat with the golden metal bat attached to the figure. He drops the trophy on the bed while watching her legs flail across the sheets, reaching with her right arm, while her left hand squeezes David's red wrinkled sleeve. With every second, her movement slows, until all stops. It's unbelievably quiet, considering the immense terror in the room.

The man walks out and down the hallway, breathing a bit harder now. He retrieves a syringe from his side pocket, filled halfway with a clear liquid. The plastic end is depressed, and a small pool of liquid sits at the bottom of his pocket. He heads into the master bedroom and, without hesitation, approaches the side and removes a large cloth bandage from his left pocket. He pours a bit of the liquid onto the cloth and, with great force, covers Tina's mouth and nose.

Her eyes open wide, and a squeak slips from the corner of her mouth.

As she passes out, John wakes to see a huge man hovering over his wife and close to him. John rolls and grabs the man's arm.

The man plunges the syringe into John's chest, piercing the heart. He pushes the plunger to release the fluid into the muscle. He falls atop them, using his chest to cover John's mouth, quieting his painful agony. The man slowly moves off the bed and sees a drowsy Tina awaken. He grabs the cloth and replaces it over her face.

She looks up and blinks, releasing a tear from the corner of her eye. Helpless, she falls into the deepest of sleep.

The man leaves the bodies without concern. Moments later, the figure enters the den. He observes Carrie laying on the couch, with Carly asleep by her feet. The blankets are falling off, and a half-full glass of water sits on the stand. Baby Jessie is fast asleep in the old crib Tina had kept throughout the years.

Carrie is dreaming; she's sitting on the beach in North Carolina, while her husband builds a sandcastle with Carly and Jessie lays on a blanket. The seawater rushes up the sand every so often, cooling the playful family's feet. Jessie cries, so Carry picks her up to settle her fuss. Jessie doesn't stop. Carrie tries with all her love to settle her down but can't. She panics a bit, and the bright sun-filled sky darkens. The wind gusts, and the view is fuzzy; nothing is recognizable. After seconds, everything is pitch black; all she hears is the crying of a scared baby.

With a jolt, Carrie awakens and quickly calms, knowing it was only a dream, then she realizes Jessie is actually crying, and it must have caused her dream. She sees Carly still asleep by her feet and turns to attend to Jessie, then gasps.

The dark figure is holding Jessie, rocking her back and forth.

Carrie screams, but there is no one to help.

With a final rock forward, the figure moves upon Carrie, and another nightmare begins.

Chapter 12

Jake wakes in his bed, half naked. He enters his bathroom to find the water running. He shuts it off and grabs his phone from the shelf. He looks at it to find the time, but it's dead. He walks downstairs and sees the pictures and files he threw across the floor. He remembers the urgent information he wanted to tell Deputy Maison. He grabs the pictures and runs to his car.

Jake gets to the station to find it vacant. He tries to call the deputy, and even the captain, but without an answer. He plugs in his phone and enters a conference room. Perusing the pictures on the board, he writes the ages of each victim. He places the name of Sonny's murdered family members underneath each picture as well.

He writes 68 next to Mrs. Webster and Grandma underneath. He writes 38 and deceased next to Mrs. Simon and 42 next to Mr. Simon, with Dad under it. He places the ages of the two missing Simon daughters in the same fashion. Now a family member's name is under each presumed missing person and deceased under all who have recently died around town. He draws new squares, the size of the photos next to the original pictures, in a straight line. He places an M or F, representing male or female, and a number for age inside each new square.

Maison and Captain Trombley enter, eye each other, and glance at Jake. "What are you doing?" they ask.

"Guys, guys. Look at this. Every person in the last week who's gone missing is the same sex and close to the age of one of Sonny's family members. All murdered either don't fit the gender or are too young or old. I think Sonny is trying to retake his family by kidnapping people who resemble those he lost. I also put on the board the demographic he would still be looking for."

Maison spies the new pictures of Sonny's murdered family, with gender and age written underneath.

Jake explains further, "Sonny would need to find two more thirtysomething women and man, a boy around thirteen, and finally, a baby girl. After comparing our recent victims, it would seem that both age and appearance will be similar."

The captain and Maison raise their eyebrows at each other.

Jake, hair greasy and messy, refocuses on the board. He is jittery, as if he drank ten cups of coffee, and the writing on the board is sloppy. Frantically trying to get his point across, he looks like a mad scientist who has been awake for days, insanely working on a masterpiece. "It's all starting to make sense. Can't you see? I've been telling you that he's alive."

Maison pounds his fist on the desk. "No! No! Nothing makes sense. This case doesn't make sense, and you don't make sense. In the last two weeks, we've had more murders and bodies than we've had in the last twenty years."

Jake glares at Maison. "Dammit, Maison. If you don't listen to me, this will all be on you!"

"Go to hell. I love you, Jake, but you're losing it!"

"Enough!" the captain shouts. "Jake, this is all very hard to figure out. We have people missing, and some brutally murdered. But if you are right, you might as well cross off four more from your list."

Jake halts and regards the captain. "What? What are you talking about?"

"Well, we've been trying to get a hold of you all day," Maison interjects. "You have been impossible to reach. But that's not here nor there; we just came from Marysville, that little town west of us where Sonny's family used to live. Their police found a family murdered—two from blunt trauma from a baseball trophy and another man stabbed with a syringe to the heart—and called us due to our recent problem. Forensics is performing tests, and we have an autopsy scheduled."

Jake sits. "This is screwed up."

Maison continues, "That's not all. The wife is missing, and it seems they had guests, but we are not sure yet. We found a crib, a stuffed bear, and a cellphone on the nightstand, indicating a possible adult. We called some of the numbers on it, but nothing. We should know who the owner is soon. It seems two females—a young girl and a baby—are missing or dead."

Jake thinks out loud, "Another young girl? But he already has the two Simon daughters, unless something happened to one of them."

Maison looks away and mumbles, "Or unless you're just wrong."

Jake sits with his head in his hands. "This is all my fault. I should've killed those bastards!"

The captain leans toward Jake. "Listen. If you're right, then there are only two victims left: a man in his thirties and a boy in his teens."

Maison quickly stands toward the captain. "You don't know that! We don't know anything!"

"No, I don't, but it's the only lead we have. Send out a description of possible targets."

Maison laughs. "Talk about a long shot."

Trombley glares at Maison. "Just do it!"

Maison leaves the room.

Trombley sits down. "Listen, Jake. What else can you tell me?"

Jake looks up with a pale, clammy expression. "I don't know. I can't sleep, can't eat, and when I do sleep, I have nightmares that are so real. I just feel so lost."

The captain puts his hand on Jake's shoulder. "We'll get through this, but is there anything else?"

Jake stops to think. "Actually I did check a hut a few days ago. I think it might be where Sonny could be staying."

The captain furrows his brows. "What? Why didn't you tell us?"

Jake looks down. "I wasn't sure. Everyone says I'm crazy."

"No, you're just trying to protect that boy; however, if he's the one doing this, he is no longer your friend, your worry, or your sadness; he's a brutal killer. Go back there

79

now. If you think he's there, call us. Jake, you do what you must. You take him out if it comes to it!"

Chapter 13

Jake speeds toward the hut on a two-lane highway and hears over the radio, "Be aware, possible victims for serial killer—men in their thirties to forties with dark complexion, teenage boys as well." He quickly turns it off, murmuring to himself, and looks in the rearview mirror. The reflection reveals a man he can't recognize, one of frantic despair. His eyes are bloodshot, and he looks sick and weak. "I'm sorry, Sonny, but I have to do what's right." He turns down the dirt road leading to the hut.

He arrives at the old structure, pulls up to a wide-open door and slowly approaches, lightly calling out, "S-Sonny? It's me. Jake. Let me take care of you." Jake, no longer sure if Sonny would not hurt him, slowly unholsters his gun. He stops at the entrance, where he can see about half of the room. "Just come over here. I only came to talk."

He discerns nothing but an eerie silence in the room, the beating of his fast-pumping heart, and the leaves crinkling in the blowing wind.

"Okay, Sonny, I'm coming in. Just be still."

Carefully maneuvering his feet, he takes one step and places his back on the wooden door. He shuffles sideways to enter the room, gun at the high ready. Nothing. He slowly turns, and something brushes his shoulder. Jake leaps backward and falls to the floor. He's on his back, with two hands gripping his pistol, aimed at the figure. It takes but only seconds to realize that a doctor's coat, hanging on the backside of the door and still swinging from when he pushed open the door, is the cause of his fright. Jake laughs, sounding like a mental patient.

He gets up and notices overturned bottles and supplies, as well as piles of coats and blankets soaked in dark stains resembling dirt and blood. "What have you done!" He swipes the gun across the supplies, sending bottles across the room, breaking on impact. He rips down the shelving unit, barely escaping the fall. He punches the door, only to split open his middle knuckle.

Outside, Jake retrieves an almost-full bottle of a fifth of whiskey from his cruiser trunk and stares at it. After much thought, he quickly twists the top, allowing it to fly off and fall to the dirt. With the gun in his left hand and the bottle in his right, he leans back and drinks. The liquid poison that he once knew too well hits the back of his throat, leaving a slight burn as it goes down, gulp after gulp. He yanks the bottle from his mouth and vomits all over the car's taillight and ground. He wipes his mouth with his shirt sleeve and blows the residual puke from his nose.

He inspects his gun and surveys the thick woods. His thoughts are empty, and his mind numb. With a tighter grip, he puts the bottle to his lips and drinks as much as his body will allow. After thirty minutes of power drinking, the alcohol overtakes him, and he shuts down, passing out near the rear the wheel of his car, gun and bottle resting near his chest.

*****

At the station, Captain Trombley pages Jake over the police car radio. "Jake, you there?" After a few tries, the captain calls Maison.

"Hey, Cap, we have the descriptions out on Sonny and the possible victims, but there hasn't been much from it."

"Listen. Jake went to that hut in the woods by the hospital. He thought Sonny might be there. I can't get a hold of him. Go there right away!"

Chapter 14

Just outside Marysville, west of the city line, sits a beautiful Civil War–period home—with a few modifications—accompanied by a small family farm. Susie and little Bella are out back, picking berries and setting some clothes on the line. Susie swears the beautiful Alabama air provides the freshest scent for clothes—well, that and her well-maintained yet overgrown flowerbed.

Bella twirls, her little dress opening like a parachute spinning in the sky. Her mom tells her if she keeps doing that, she'll fall and get hurt. She laughs it off, a simple innocent soul. She resumes filling the fruit basket.

*****

A few miles down the road, Aaron drives his rusted Ford truck, with Harry riding along. A football helmet and shoulder pads rest against a half-empty water bottle in the rear. The father and son discuss practice, until a large figure emerges in the distance.

Aaron pulls alongside. "Hello there, sir. Can I help you?"

The man strides forward without a reply.

"Sir? You need a ride or to make a call?"

The man traverses the road with his chin dug into his chest and face hidden.

The boys in the truck are hungry and impatient, so Aaron speeds away.

"That was weird," Harry exclaims.

"Yeah," Aaron replies.

"See, Harry. That's why you gotta stay in school."

Harry laughs. "Yeah, Dad. No doubt!"

"Maybe I'll give Sheriff Donaldson a call," Aaron says. "I think I saw his squad car at the diner a few miles back. So anyway, you ready for some supper?"

*****

The day grows dim, and Deputy Maison arrives at the shed. He exits the car and sees the empty bottle of whiskey. He moves inside to see the wreckage. He brushes a few things with his boot, and a light from outside beams into his eyes. He bends to find a picture of Sonny and his family on a summer day. To the right, he notices the stained coats and T-shirt. He looks up to find syringes and medical supplies. He remembers the victim with the stab wound to the heart.

Maison gets to the radio. "Captain."

Trombley comes through the speaker, "I'm here. Go on."

"Jake's not here, his car is gone, the hut is a mess, and it looks like a good hideout. A lot of the murders could be traced to these objects."

"I'll notify the chief and surrounding towns. You locate Jake ASAP!"

*****

Aaron and Harry pull up the driveway as Bella runs around the back. They step out. Harry grabs his stuff and heads inside to shower. Aaron walks out back.

"Daddy, Daddy!" Bella runs and jumps into his arms.

He gives her a big hug and approaches Susie. "Hi, hun." He gives her a kiss. "Oh, those look good. You gonna make that famous jam of yours?"

Susie smiles and gives a playful smirk, knowing her jams are too tart. "Oh yeah, and I'll enjoy watching you eat the whole jar."

They both giggle.

Susie asks, "Can you help me put the stuff away?"

Aaron replies, "Sure can."

"Me too, me too. I can help," Bella yells.

Aaron and Susie laugh. "Okay, Bella, you can help too."

Harry is inside, getting ready to shower. The steam from the hot water rolls over the curtain. He passes through the hallway to his room for some clothes and hears the kitchen door open and close. He yells downstairs, "Hey, Mom, did you wash my shorts?" He pauses. "Mom? Dad?"

Harry, with a towel wrapped around his waist, heads downstairs and enters the kitchen to find it vacant. He swings open the door to see his family picking up some final things. "Hey, Mom, Dad, did you hear me?"

Susie replies, "What?"

"Did you wash the shorts I had on the floor?"

"Oh, yes. They are probably done in the dryer."

Harry releases the door, hearing the same sound it just made moments ago. He carefully descends to the basement, trying to keep his towel up and tight. The cement is cool, and a musty smell fills the air. The basement is unfinished and stocked with memories. Boxes of pictures and toys are scattered throughout. Harry walks to the dryer, bypassing the string hanging from the light fixture. Light from the porch and garage comes through the basement window, offering just enough to discern the laundry area.

Harry bends to open the dryer door, not noticing the strange addition in the corner, and reaches in for the white-and-red mesh shorts. The bright light illuminates the space behind him, leaving his shadow on the back wall. As the door begins to shut, a faint brushing sound comes to his right. With a startling jerk, the door latch closes, and he stands erect, facing the corner. His breath stops, and he becomes motionless; he wants to move, but the shock has frozen him. He stares at the large body in the corner but can't decipher the figure. He's still fairly blinded from the bright dryer light, and now the once-lit room is pitch dark.

"Harry?" his mom yells down. "Did you find them?"

Harry breaks from his trance. "Yeah. Hey, hold on!" Harry bounds up the steps.

"Is everything all right?" Susie asks, one eyebrow raised.

"Oh, forget it," Harry answers, not wanting to share his silly startle from what surely must be just a common noise from an old basement.

"Okay, well, go shower. It's dinnertime."

*****

Deputy Maison has been driving around for hours, not finding anything helpful. Unable to reach Jake by phone or car radio, he checks in at the station. "Hey, you there?"

After a moment, the captain comes over the radio, "Yeah, Maison, I'm here. Do you have anything?"

"No, not really. I've been driving around for almost two hours and haven't seen anything suspicious. Madison Police called, though, to say they received a report from a resident about a strange guy walking the streets. They said they wanted to let us know because of the things happening around the local towns. I'm gonna check it out. It's probably just a hitchhiker, but I don't have anything else to do."

"Yeah, there hasn't been much on our end, either. Some detectives searched the hut and agree someone has recently occupied it, and they're dusting for prints. Luckily, we still have some prints on file from the hospital records. They can't confirm, however, if any equipment in the hut was used for the murders. Just take a quick look in Madison and come back to town. We need everyone on the streets to make the community feel safe."

"You got it."

*****

At the farmhouse, Harry washes each dinner dish, then hands it to Bella for the final dry off.

"See. I can do big girl stuff."

"Of course, you can," Harry warmly confirms, while they work the dishes.

Susie and Aaron secretly discuss their surprise vacation to Disney World. Aaron leans back in his warm recliner, lifting the leg rest. "Well, I think we have just enough to do it. We'll stay at the hotel for five days and spend another two at Disney. I can't wait to see the look on Bella's face."

"You know Harry is gonna love it, too. He's been helping us around here so much lately that he really needs a break. If we can only pry him from that girlfriend of his."

They both laugh.

"Hey, what's so funny?" Harry asks as he and Bella walk in.

Susie looks up. "Oh, nothing. The dishes done?"

Bella proudly responds, "Clean as a whistle."

Susie reclines in her chair. "Oh, okay, you big girl, go get washed up. I'll be there to tuck you in. You go too, Harry. You have another big day tomorrow."

*****

Moments later, Susie tucks in Bella. "Sweet dreams. I'll see you tomorrow, but did you say your prayers?"

"Oh no! I forgot!" Bella turns quickly and folds her hands. "Now I lay me down to sleep, I pray the Lord my soul to keep. If I die before I wake, I pray the Lord my soul to take. God bless Mommy, Daddy, Harry, Mrs. Smith, Kitty, that frog in the stream, the birdies ..."

Susie giggles as she closes the door.

Harry fills his bedtime glass of water in the kitchen and wipes the side where a drop slides down. He looks out the window. The night is calm, and everything is in place. He turns and slowly closes the still-cracked-open basement door. Each stair creaks as he climbs the steps toward his room.

In the bedroom, an exhausted Susie climbs under the sheets.

Aaron turns over and kisses her. "Goodnight, hun. Love you. Have a great day tomorrow."

Susie, almost halfway asleep, replies, "Love you too."

*****

The night is still. Maison cruises the lonely Madison streets. "Cap, this is Maison. Over."

A voice from the radio responds, "Come in."

"I'm heading back. I've been driving for a while and haven't seen anything or anyone in this town. Has anyone found Jake?"

"No. We sent a car to his house. The neighbors believe they saw him earlier but aren't sure.

Check in if you find anything. I want you back patrolling here soon."

*****

Whoosh! The whistling of the wind wraps around the farmhouse. The gusts occasionally tap the shutters against the house. Inside, an ominous calm has settled; it's very dark and so quiet that the faint buzzing of electrical appliances fills the air. Upstairs, Harry and Bella are fast asleep in their rooms. Bella's angel nightlight illuminates her face, and her favorite blanket is tucked under her arms. In the master bedroom on the main floor, Susie soundly sleeps in a warm, oversized bed, with layers of covers atop her. She doesn't know she's sleeping alone.

Aaron has snuck outside to the barn to work on his big surprise. A couple nights a week, he sneaks out to work on the walnut porch swing Susie has always wanted, adorned with elaborate carvings of their past together. On the back rest, he engraved a maple tree, with a heart on its trunk, resembling their first kiss. Each armrest holds the names Bella and Harry. It's a beautiful piece of art that he can hang tomorrow if he puts in just enough work.

* * * * *

Downstairs in the damp, musty room, sounds emerge. "Ten, nine, eight, seven, six, five, try to stay alive. Four, just three counts more. Three, better hide from me. Two, I'm coming for you. One, let's have some fun!"

The figure slowly rises, with his back resting on the corner walls. He stands there for a moment to collect his balance. One small lean forward provides enough weight transfer to move ahead. With each step closer to the stairs, he regains his strength, and his dark heart beats faster, filling his body with demon blood. He feels energized and powerful.

He ascends the stairs to the kitchen and heads to the living room, not noticing the barn light on. As he enters the room, his foot catches on a long, coiled cord. His gaze follows the cord to an old white wall phone. With a quick tug, he rips the cord from the receiver. He travels through the living room to the staircase, passing the master bedroom, which is a bit hidden to the side. He grabs the staircase railing to pull his body one step at a time.

At the top, he slowly opens a bedroom door to expose little Bella snug in bed. The man sits next to her and gazes for a moment, unsure why he's there. He pets her head and moves his fingers through her hair.

Bella takes a long, deep breath, waking from her slumber. She turns and looks at him.

He smiles at her while caressing her head.

Bella wipes her eyes. "Daddy?"

The man smiles and continues caressing her.

"Daddy, Daddy?" Her hazy vision dissipates, and she realizes a stranger is on her bed. She wails, "Mommy—"

The man places his hand over her mouth. The scream woke him from his daze; he remembers the screams from the past, and it enrages him. He panics, looking for anything to quiet her with.

She squirms, like a desperate fish out of water.

He quickly stands to grab the porcelain doll off the dresser.

Bella screams.

He returns to the bed, lifts his hand, and thrusts it down.

Just as the doll is about to strike, Harry dives across the room and forces the man into the nightstand. Harry yells to Bella, "Run!"

But she can't move; the unwelcome stranger has a tight grip on her wrist.

The two struggle, but Harry can't keep him down. The man pulls Bella to the floor and stands. Harry grabs the doll on the bed and strikes the man in the head. Blood dribbles down the invader's cheek and neck. Enraged, the man grabs Harry's neck and squeezes.

Bella slides under the bed, frozen from fear, and is silent, hoping the man will forget she is there.

After a moment, Harry falls unconscious from the lack of oxygen and, with little life, passes to the floor.

Susie, downstairs, wakes but is not sure why. Did she hear Bella? She sits upright and swings her legs over the edge, collecting her thoughts.

The man grabs Harry's legs and pulls him to the stairs, then drags the unconscious body behind him. With every step, Harry's head bangs on the wood planks.

After hearing the second bang, Susie enters the still-dark living room. She sees the dark figure but isn't awake enough to understand. She loudly calls out, "Aaron? What are you doing?"

Bella hears her mom and slides from underneath the bed. She runs to the staircase, screaming, "Mom! Help Harry. Help!"

Susie flips the light switch to a surreal sight. Her mind can't put the pieces together fast enough.

Bella runs to the steps. "Leave Harry alone!" She bends over and grabs Harry's arm and tries to pull him up.

Susie realizes her worst fear and belts a curdling scream.

Aaron, in the barn, looks up when he hears the cry and sprints toward the house, holding the wood-carving chisel.

Susie runs to the foot of the stairs and throws everything in sight.

Bella, still tugging, is pulled down each step with Harry.

Susie grabs the man and tries to pull him down.

He kicks her stomach, catapulting her to the floor.

"Stop!" Bella climbs his back and grabs his neck.

He releases Harry and tries to grab Bella. Unable to get her, he turns his back to the staircase wall and leaps backward to squish her between the wall and his body. When she lets go, he turns and grabs her neck.

Susie, already risen, races up the stairs. She hits his arms to help Bella, but he's too strong and whips Bella's little body around and over the railing.

Bella's foot catches the wood rail, flipping her to fall headfirst to the floor.

The loud clunk on the living room floor brings Susie to her knees. She looks over the railing, barely seeing through tear-stained eyes. "No! Nooooo!" A final exhausted cry escapes her mouth with a shaking, quivering tone.

Aaron emerges to behold the scene: the man on the staircase, Harry laying on the steps, and Susie's face, with tears and snot hanging from her lips, poking through the railing posts. He notices his little girl, motionless on the floor.

Susie cries with little breath, "Where were you?"

The man punches his palm to the back of Susie's head, forcing it through the two staircase posts. Her head is stuck.

Aaron narrows his gaze on the familiar dark figure. "You! I'm gonna kill you!" He races to the stairs, clenching his chisel. He plunges upward but has a disadvantage.

They struggle a bit, and Harry awakens. Harry, with little strength, kicks the man in the calf.

Startled, the man loses grip with Aaron, and in one motion, Aaron tries to shove the sharp metal into the devil's abdomen but slips, barley cutting him and leaving the chisel jammed into the wall. The man loses footing and tumbles backward.

Aaron turns to help Susie from the post. It's so tight, and blood runs down from where the beam ripped her ear. "I'm so sorry. I'm so sorry!"

With no time to comfort anyone, Harry yells, "Dad, look out!"

The man, having pulled the chisel from the wall, leans forward to stab Aaron. Upon hearing Harry's cry, he sidesteps out of the way. The chisel misses Aaron, traveling just underneath his arm, but drives into Susie's back.

She belts a sharp scream, the tremendous pain more than she could have ever imagined.

Aaron pushes the man backward and tries to grab the weapon lodged in her back. With one powerful kick, the man sends Aaron sideways down the stairs. His leg twists, and his knee pops before he comes to rest at the bottom of the staircase. "Leave them alone, please. Leave them alone!"

The demonic figure hovers over Susie's stuck body, takes a deep breath, and kicks the bottom post sandwiching Susie's head. It breaks and releases her.

Susie leans over and slowly slides down the steps, every inch sending splintering pain through her.

Harry tries to get up, but he's just too dizzy.

The man punches the side of Harry's head, knocking him out, and pulls Harry the rest of the way down the stairs.

Susie watches, half out of life. "Please, please stop. Please."

Aaron tries to move, but his broken leg makes it unbearable.

The man binds Harry's and Aaron's wrists and ankles with rope he found in the basement. Harry is still unconscious, and Aaron can barely slide his leg. The man ties Susie to the coffee table; she's too weak to move anyway. He turns off the light and leaves.

In a dark room, drowning with confusion and pain, Aaron whispers, "Harry? Susie? God, Susie, oh God, please be okay!"

Susie is between life and death; she can barely decipher her loving husband's voice. She releases a very low sigh.

Aaron hears life slowly leaving her body. "Honey, I'm so sorry I wasn't here for us," he says with a whimper. "I just wanted to make something for you, something we could share forever." He describes the swing to her in full detail, hoping she might have one last happy memory, as a small tear falls from his eye.

With every ounce of remaining strength, Susie pushes out one last whispered breath. "I love you."

Aaron squeezes his hands. "I love you too." He bellows in despair.

Harry feels cold, and although he is alive, he appears lifeless. Awakened by Aaron's yell, he moves.

"Harry? Harry?" Aaron cries out. "Wake up!"

It takes a few moments, but Harry regains consciousness. "What's going on, Dad?"

"Son, we gotta get out of here."

Harry looks around. "Where's Mom? Where's Bella?"

"You can't worry about that right now. We have to go."

"Tell me what happened!"

"Son ... they're gone."

"No!" Harry feverishly wiggles and jolts.

Aaron joins the desperate dance of delusion, knowing he can't break free.

"I got it," Harry says with a grunt. "I just have to ..." The rope loosens from his wrist. He slips from his hand restraints and, dizzy and nauseated, frantically works on his ankles.

"Harry, just calm down."

Harry takes a deep breath. After a few tries, he loosens the rope and turns to free his dad.

"No. Don't worry about me. Go call the police."

Harry runs to the kitchen and places the receiver to his ear. He flicks the switch hook a few times. "There's nothing, Dad!"

"He must have cut the cord."

Harry runs to his dad to free him, knowing that's the only phone in the house, and works on the knot around Aaron's ankle.

"Wait. The barn! Go use the phone in the barn."

Harry stops. "Shit, that's right! Okay, I'll be right back." He runs through the doorway into the kitchen and grabs a knife. He sees the barn through the window. He yanks open the back door, and it slams against the inside kitchen wall. He runs across gravel and grass in his bare feet to reach the barn and find the phone. He lifts the receiver and dials 9-1-1.

"What's your emergency?"

"My family has been killed. 4687 Elmira Drive. Hurry!" Harry leaves the receiver off the hook and rushes to help his dad. He raises the kitchen knife, pushes open the barn's screen door, and—whack! A tire iron strikes Harry's face, and he crumples to the ground.

While Harry's body keeps the barn door ajar, the man returns to the living room.

Aaron closes his eyes, knowing all hope is lost.

Chapter 15

In another town, just miles away, Deputy Maison radios the station.

"Go ahead, Maison."

"Marysville Police contacted me five minutes ago. They received a call from a kid who lives on that street I was patrolling earlier today. The kid said his family had been killed. I'm on my way there right now. We don't know if he called while the killer was there or if the killer had just left. Send units. I'll be there in about fifteen minutes."

Maison arrives at the house and parks alongside two Marysville Police cars. He sees two officers in the house and one out back, with a flashlight; the morning is breaking, but the sun is just reaching the horizon. Maison enters.

"We're too late. The boy and father are gone. We only found Mrs. Findlay, dead on the floor from a stab wound to her lower back. We found their daughter lying over here."

Maison kneels, bracing his shivering body. "Hey there, sweetie. Are you okay?"

Bella sits at the end of the couch, wrapped in blankets.

An officer replies, "Yeah, she's okay. She broke her leg. Medics have taken good care of her. They'll question her at the hospital. I called you in to see if this made any sense, or if she could answer a question for you; however, she hasn't said anything yet. The shock has paralyzed her."

Maison looks into the little girl's eyes. "Sweetie, my name is Deputy Maison. Do you remember anything?" He waits a moment. "It's okay." Maison looks up. "Tell me what you think happened."

A taller officer turns and tilts back his hat. He pulls a notepad from his pocket. "The husband and son are missing. We have no idea if they're alive. We received the call about thirty minutes ago and arrived about fifteen minutes after the call. You know how big this county is. Anyway, we came through the front and found Mrs. Findlay, dead, lying right here next to these chairs. I went upstairs and found the girl's room a mess, like a struggle and, as you can see, blood all over the steps and wall and these two broken posts. My partner found Bella. We checked the basement and located the barn phone off its hook. We found blood on the doorframe. Another officer arrived and is now checking outside. We were hoping you could help figure this out; obviously we know what's been going on."

"My partner, Deputy Keller, has a theory, and it looks like he might be right. If he is, that means our suspect, Sonny, kidnapped Mr. Findlay and their son. It seems Sonny is trying to reunite his murdered family from the nineteen seventy-eight massacre by kidnapping people who resemble his family members. How Bella is alive, I have no idea."

"Well, we found her barely conscious. He must have thought she was dead."

"That makes sense."

A figure walks through the kitchen and into the room.

The three officers regard him, and one asks, "Find anything out there?"

"I looked all around. There's no indication of a forced entry, almost as if our killer was inside all along. I found two tire tracks leading out the front, and the family's truck is missing."

The officer furrows his brows at Maison. "That freak knows how to drive?"

Maison nods. "Yeah. Some worker at the hospital used to take him to a hut in the woods. He must have taught him."

"Shit. We need to check that hut," an officer replied.

"I already did today. It looks like it's been used, but with all the missing people, he must be somewhere else."

The officer looks at his partner. "We need to find this asshole! This is a bunch of bullshit, and where is this Jake of yours? The man who protected this little prick his whole life?"

Maison points at the officer. "Hey, you listen to me. That man has gone through more than you could ever, in three lifetimes. Don't you ever disrespect him again!"

The officer, calmer, repeats, "Where is he?"

Maison puts his hands atop his head, while he shakes it. "I don't know. He searched the hut, too, and hasn't been seen since." Maison omits the empty whiskey bottle from the story to protect Jake. "I'm sure he is doing everything he can to find the bastard."

Another officer interrupts, "Alright! Alright already. Enough! I'm sorry. We're just trying to figure this out. We'll stay here until the detectives arrive. I'd rather see you out there, finding this freak, but you can look around."

"Fine. I'll do that, then I'll go." Maison approaches the staircase and observes evidence to suggest that most of the struggle happened there—the broken rail posts, blood on the steps and the wall, the chipped paint, and scrapes. Knowing he can't do anything else now, he just wants to find this little girl's brother and father.

Chapter 16

An hour later, Maison sits in his car, mentally exhausted from the scene. He radios the police station to inform the captain of what happened and that the paramedics are transporting the little girl to the hospital, alive.

The captain wants him to return to piece together everything they know and to decide what to do next.

As Maison prepares to sign off, his phone flashes, indicating a missed call. He clicks the button and sees Jake called minutes ago. He tells the captain and dials Jake's number, trying to figure out what to say. His anger boils over, knowing Jake was drunk during this last murder.

"Hello? Maison?"

Maison retorts, "Yeah. Where the hell are you?"

A quiet voice comes across the phone. "I-I'm not sure. I just woke up in my car a little while ago. I think I'm just outside of town. My head is pounding. Maison, I'm really sorry. I kind of drank last night."

"I know. I found the bottle at the hut, near the pond."

"Oh … I guess I'm just hungover."

"While you were passed out, Sonny killed again!"

As if an ice-cold bucket of water hit him, Jake's voice sounds crisp, clear. "What? No. Not again!"

"Yeah, a farmhouse in Marysville. You were right; he kidnapped a man and his son."

"I'll be right there!"

"No, there's no use. I just left." Jake's breathing wrestles through the phone speaker. "Oh my God, I'm so sorry."

"Well, even though you did screw up, you couldn't have stopped it anyway."

Jake pauses. "A man and his son? If that's the case, he has finished. He has them all. We will never find him—wait, what about the hut?"

"No, he couldn't go there; we have it under surveillance. If he has all these people, he must be hiding them somewhere. The hospital is abandoned, but it's all open, and someone would have seen something."

Both men sit quietly, thinking, until Jake excitedly says, "The house!"

"What? What house?"

"The house where Sonny grew up, the house where this all began."

"Are you telling me that no one has been there?" Maison exclaimed.

"We did. We checked it after the hospital burned down. It was just a cold, abandoned home. We could tell no one had been there since the massacre. Maybe Sonny was using the hut but recently returned to the house to hide his new family. Let's meet at the station and group up."

"I'll call the captain and let him know what's going on." Maison throws the phone onto the passenger seat cushion, mashes the accelerator, and radios the station.

Captain Trombley answers the incoming transmission. "What the hell is going on? Where's Jake?"

"I'll let him explain that to you later, but right now, we're meeting at the station, before going to Sonny's childhood home. We think it's where he's keeping all his victims."

"I'll notify Marysville PD."

Maison drops the radio and peers through the windshield. All he can do is pray they find the victims—and hopefully alive. His tires squeal over the hot pavement as he speeds away.

*****

In another car, racing toward the police station, a steering wheel vibrates from the constant pounding of a fist. Jake is livid at himself. His stomach aches from the booze and the guilt, retching over and over. All he wants is for this to stop, and he hopes this will be the last time he has to deal with it. He holsters his gun, and a deep chill overcomes him.

He slams on the brakes and stops his car, angled on the road. "No, this ends now." He violently spins the steering wheel to redirect toward the old farmhouse he wishes he never knew.

*****

Half an hour later, at the station, Maison enters. "Where's Jake?"

Captain Trombley shrugs. "I thought you were meeting here."

Maison slams his fist on the table. "Yes, we are! But he should be here already. You don't think ... Shit, I bet he went straight to the house. Captain, would you stay here as our communications post and call Marysville Police to tell them where I'm headed? They'll be about forty minutes behind me, but I need the backup in case Sonny is there. I just don't think Jake will know how to handle him."

Maison ensures his gun is on his duty belt and grabs another clip from the desk. He races from the building, forgetting to grab his protective vest. He knows Jake is probably at the farm by now, and time is ticking. He jumps into the car and speeds away.

Chapter 17

At the farm, Jake exits the vehicle. The wind blows cool air across his face. Leaves pass by, nicking his sleeves. The house structurally looks the same, just old. The paint has all but weathered away, and rust has oxidized the metal fixtures to a maroon color. He steps very quietly, listening for any commotion. As he approaches the side of the house, his memories play out, like a silent black-and-white movie, of Vern and his crew killing the men by the grill, then the shotgun blast that mowed down two children, and the insane murder of a grandmother and grandchild.

Jake passes the corner to the back. He studies the cornfield and remembers the small face of a child viewing the massacre in total fear. The memories make his head pinch. Aching from the front of his skulls travels backward. The daylight burns his eyes. Vomit approaches his throat, but he forces it down. The burning in his chest forces the pain and memories in his head to soften. He takes a deep breath and remembers why he's there.

While investigating the side of the house, he doesn't see or hear anyone. The wind gusts, and windchimes ring in the distance. Jake spots rusted-silver tubes banging against each other, then notices a bunch of hay stacks and what looks like a wooden pallet near the clearing by the dried-out cornfield, just about one hundred feet from the house—something he hadn't noticed before. The wind must have blown the hay off it since the last time he was there. He gets closer and sees the dirt has been roughed up and the grass is missing. He reaches down to slide the wood, but it won't slide; it's hinged. He lifts the wood to expose a cavern. All that is visible is a set of eight steps. He begins down, crouching as low as he can to see the dirt floor.

The underground world is pitch dark.

Chapter 18

Maison, only a mile from the house, prepares himself for the unknown. The inertia of the lefthand turn pushes his body to the right, and the car bounces off a pothole dug into the entrance of the driveway. As he creeps the car toward the house, he feels the dark energy grow. Jake's car sits near the house, but Maison doesn't see him around. Dammit, Jake, I know you want to stop Sonny, but why couldn't you have waited?

Maison stops the car and gets out, his hand hovering over his sidearm, then proceeds to the back.

*****

Underneath the soil, a passage connects the cellar to the home. A few small dark rooms connect to each other, like a passing chamber. Jake, who already entered the space, trudges through the maze of clutter and support beams. He slowly emerges into a final large room. As he approaches the once silent dungeon, he hears moans and muffled cries from the cloth-covered mouths of its victims. He spots two tied women lying on the floor, their eyes barely open, a little girl in the corner next to a boy, and an old woman slumped over a chair.

The room spins. Flashes of the past rip through his head, a tidal wave drowning his clarity. He can only think about the tragedy of the past. He tries to calm himself, attending to his breathing and heart rate. His vision slowly improves, and he discerns a swaddled baby on the old woman's lap. A humming sound directs his gaze to a father and son bound together. The veins in the father's neck protrude as he tries to break free. The sights and sounds of the people and their muffled pain again bring him back to that July day.

He envisions the blood and the bits of flesh flying everywhere and the ear-piercing screams he hears every night as he goes to bed. In his mind, he watches a little boy die inside, witnessing the death of his family.

The room still spins, but he approaches one of the women and yanks down the cloth covering her mouth. As her eyes open, the nausea from the spinning room overtakes Jake, his knees become even weaker, and his head cramps with pain. A sound makes him turn for a split second, but nothing's there. He refocuses on the woman, whose eyes are wide and pupils enlarged, indicating she could finally see his face in front of her.

She releases a curdling scream.

The high-pitched scream and pressure from his head causes Jake to black out, and all sounds fade.

*****

When the scream barely reaches Maison's ears at the surface, he frantically searches for a passage. After a moment, he finds a wooden plank protruding from a pile of hay that the intense wind covered. He brushes off the top to expose the wooden door and carefully descends the creaking steps into the dark room. His eyes adjust while his sweaty hand grips his gun.

Maison enters the next room, with the pistol at the low ready. With each step, his anxiety increases, and faint sounds intensify. He creeps into the final room. A candle's flickering flame dances the shadows of bodies against the walls. There's no sign of Jake anywhere. He takes a few more steps and sees the boy and father, recognizing them from the pictures at the farmhouse.

He approaches and places his hand on the man's shoulder. "I'm gonna get you out, but I want you to know your little girl is—"

Aaron belts a fierce moan through the cloth covering his mouth.

Maison begins to turn, and—whack!—something strikes the back of his head, and he collapsed to the ground.

Chapter 19

Screeching, wrestling, grunting, moaning—all these sounds fill the room. Not knowing how much time has elapsed, Maison awakens. Every little sound pierces him. His head pounds, but the candlelit room helps him progressively see. After composing himself, he turns his head toward the noise and sees a man bent over near the old woman.

Maison whispers, "Who's there?" but his voice is too weak to hear. He tries again. "What happened?"

The wrestling sound stops.

Maison rubs his head. "Did we save them?"

The large man faces Maison and says softly, "I'm sorry, Jake. I know you tried really hard, but guess what? I got my family back." The man's voice is deep, like an adult, but his speech resembles that of a child.

Maison's eyes widen in confusion. He notices a small pipe on the ground, only feet away, with what looks like blood splattered on it. Blood also speckles the man's sleeve. A rush of adrenaline explodes from Maison's heart, and he focuses on the man. "You? You hit me?"

The deep voice replies, "I had to, Jake. I know you wanted to stop me. I have my family now, and now we can be happy."

Maison raises an eyebrow. "Why do you keep calling me Jake? This is not your family!"

"This is my family now! You have always been there for me, but you didn't save them! It's your fault. It's all your fault!"

Maison looks ahead at the ropes and chains holding up the old woman in her chair. The baby lies still in the woman's lap. It appears fresh makeup covers the old lady's face. He notices colored powder covering the man's fingers. "Now calm down. You're right; it is my fault. I'm sorry. Don't you know I never mean to hurt you?"

With a slow subtle change, the man relaxes his aggressive stance. "Of course, you took care of me. You always came to see me, and you're my family, too. I love you, Jake!"

Maison, with a low voice, replies, "Yeah, I love you too, but what are you doing with these people? Why don't we let them go, and we can go home?"

"No. This is my family. They don't want to go!"

Maison nods in agreement. "Okay, okay."

The man turns to continue painting the old woman's face.

Through the reflection of a mirror next to him, Maison spots a gun lying on a table alongside the many colors of makeup and stands. "Why don't I hold the baby while you do that?"

The deep voice answers, "No, it's okay. Grandma has her."

Maison sees that the baby's clothes are sewn to the woman's blanket and holding the baby in place. The woman appears to have been dead for some time. Maison examines closer and realizes the baby is only asleep. Knowing he might have little time, he quickly reaches to his side but grabs an empty holster.

The man spies Maison through the reflection. "You're not trying to hurt me, are you?"

"Of course not. I want to help you, Sonny. I just can't find my gun. You know that's my job, right? Have you seen it?"

"Of course. It's right over here."

"Oh great, you found it. Thanks." Maison inches toward the table, breathing heavily.

The man keeps painting.

Maison takes another step and reaches for his gun.

A deep voice whispers, "I wish it was different. I wish you didn't want to hurt me."

Maison desperately lunges forward and grabs the gun. When he turns, he feels a fierce, sharp burn in his stomach and sees the metal end of a paintbrush has pierced him. He falls backward into the mirror, shattering pieces to the ground.

The enraged figure hovers over him.

Maison slowly grabs the brush and pulls out the sharp end, grunting loudly.

"Why? Why do you want to hurt me?" The man lifts his arms in anger. "Whyyy?"

Terrified, Maison clenches his fists to block himself from what he can only imagine will be a fatal blow. His left hand closes on a weighted object, rough and ridged—the grip of his pistol. The sharp pain momentarily made him forget he'd grabbed it. Maison points it at the man's chest.

The man lunges toward him.

"I'm so sorry!" As Maison squeezes the trigger, he closes his eyes, and tears streak his face. Pop, pop! Maison opens his eyes to see the man hit the ground.

*****

The man lies on his side, blood pooling near his chest. He stares at his reflection in the broken mirror that the bullet shattered moments ago, leaving a large piece stuck in the frame. A warm, calm feeling travels through his body. A smile grows on his face as he sees the reflection of the man who looked after him all these years, the man who came to the hospital and spent time when no one else was around.

His body weakens. With a final inhale, he says, "Hi, Jake. I did it. I found my family. Thanks for being my friend." He smiles, then the expression fades. A final breath escapes his mouth. As he slowly dies, he's comforted in believing he's dying alongside his only friend. He doesn't realize that he, himself, is that man in the reflection. He has no concept of the pain or the sheer terror he's caused.

*****

Maison holds his wound. "Goodbye, Jake."

The sounds of sirens appear in the distance.

Chapter 20

The next day, Maison lies in bed at the local hospital.

"Knock, knock." The door opens, and Captain Trombley enters with an unfamiliar female.

Maison tries to sit up.

"Get your ass back down." The captain laughs. "Boy oh boy, looks like you're gonna get anything you want for a while."

"I did my job. I just wish it was different. I don't understand what happened."

The captain regards the woman. "Let me introduce Dr. Therese McDay. I think she can help explain."

"Hi, Maison. I hope you're feeling better."

"I am. I just want to know what happened to Jake."

"Over the years, Jake harbored a large amount of guilt that harmed his mind. He couldn't help but think everything was his fault. After his wife and kids left, his guilt and depression turned to anger. He kept stable for some time by coming to work every day and visiting Sonny. But the day Sonny died in that fire, it triggered an explosion of desperation. You could easily notice the wear and sleep deprivation in his personality. He began having night terrors, until one night his emotions and insomnia won. He developed a split personality, one that could go in and out. It seems from the murders that this flip occurred at night when he had nightmares or when something happened to alter his mind."

Maison raises an eyebrow. "Oh, like the day when he drank and passed out?"

"Yes, that's correct. You see, when he was Jake, he acknowledged his own existence and that of Sonny. However, when he flipped, believing he was Sonny, he actively became him. His guilt and split personality led him to create his own personality of Sonny, one where he wanted to find the family members he had lost. He committed these murders and kidnappings to try to reunite them. In the underground hideout, when he believed himself to be Sonny, he may have thought you were actually him, because of your police uniform." She exhales. "It's so very sad, but you did what you had to do."

Maison looks down. "Yeah, he was calling me Jake, and once I realized something was wrong, I called him Sonny. That seemed to calm him down."

The doctor nods. "Yes, which makes sense. Please come see me if you ever want to talk or if you need anything."

The doctor left, and Trombley sits near the bed. "You better get well soon. You have a lot of work ahead."

Maison looks up. "What? What are you talking about?"

"I've seen more terrible things recently to last ten lifetimes. It's time to retire. I guess I can wait a few days till you get back, since you'll be running things, of course."

Maison, with a surprised expression, mutters, "What? You're kidding me?"

The captain flips a metal badge onto his bed, which reads, CAPTAIN MAISON STONE. "I know you're the right man for the job."

Maison smirks. "What's that in your hand?"

"Oh yeah. Well, that little girl, Bella, from the farmhouse, is staying here, too, for a few days. Her pop is pretty injured and can't see her yet. He gave me this bear to give to her. I just came from her room. I tried talking to her and said this was from her papa. Maison, she just laid there silent, staring at the ceiling. I hope she comes to."

Maison nods.

The captain pats Maison's leg and leaves the room, closing the door behind him.

*****

Down the hallway, Bella lies motionless and peacefully quiet in her bed as the TV plays commercials. The show begins with kids at the park, laughing and running around.

One of the kids on the TV yells, "Ready or not, here I come!"

Made in the USA
Columbia, SC
21 May 2024

35926388R00075